# Shattered Echoes

Stella Mace

# Copyright

# Also by Stella Mace

**Alex Harper Mystery Series**
Shrouded Deception

**Mia Conrad Mystery Series**
Shattered Echoes

**Parker Rose Mystery Series**
Small Town Shadows
Small Town Secrets

**Standalone**
Silence of Secrets

# Chapter 1:

My concentration is absolute as I try to pinpoint the location of the arms dealer I have been tracking for the last few days, my sweat causing my hands to slip on the keyboard every now and again. Whoever this is, they know how to cover their tracks, but not well enough to hide from me. With each layer of their security that I breach, my excitement builds, and my determination becomes more solid, an unbreachable and ironclad wall.

As the youngest hacker to ever be recruited to the FBI, now working at the New York field office, I love this type of challenge: finding a crooked needle in a stack of needles.

Biting my lip, I attack the sixth firewall, throwing everything I have at it.

"Package for you, Conrad."

I almost leap out of my chair as the envelope thumps down next to me on the desk.

"What the hell, O'Donnell?! Did no one teach you how to knock?"

I feel the blood rush to my face from the fright as O'Donnell grins at me, leaning against the door frame of my office, looking for all the world like a cat that stole all the cream, never mind just a bowl. He knows I shut off from the world when I concentrate on my work and makes a point of pranking or frightening me at least once a week. Some field agents think they are the absolute shit while we lowly hackers, or any office worker, for that matter, are there for their entertainment.

"Whoops. Sorry, Conrad," he drawls. "The front desk asked me to drop off the envelope as the messenger said it was urgent, and I thought, why not do my favorite colleague a favor? So, here I am, helping out."

I glower at him, pushing the envelope aside.

"Thanks," I grind out past my teeth, wishing for all the world that someone would shoot him already. Not anything serious, of course, just bad enough that I could get a week or two without him in the office. Trying to calm my heart rate, I continue, "I need to get back to work if there is nothing else."

O'Donnell knows I am seeing red as he smiles at me, lazily looking about, taking his time to reply.

"Nothing else. Only stopped in for the envelope and a quick check-in." His grin widens as he pushes himself off the door frame. "Tootles, and good luck with your little project."

Prick. Maybe I should shoot him in the foot myself, even if it's just to show him that he is not God's gift to women as he so clearly believes.

Turning my attention back to my computer, I pop the envelope in my "in" tray; it can wait a bit. I need to get back to this arms dealer before they destroy any more lives. There will be no escaping for them today.

"Conrad! Have you heard a single word I said? Why are you still at the office at this time of night?"

My head whips up as Director Angie West glares down at me, still at my desk, looking worse for wear. It had been a tough day as an undercover agent had gone missing. I look around, finally noticing that the rest of the office is empty of the normal buzz, with only a lone janitor sweeping the floors.

"Apologies, Angie. I mean Director. I, uhm... I..." I stutter as I try to find my bearings, try to remember where I am. "No, I didn't hear you. Would you mind repeating the question?"

Angie, who understands me better than anyone else, sighs loudly, not trying to conceal her tiredness and worry as she walks into my office, closing the door behind her to ensure the janitor cannot overhear us. She sinks into one of the chairs in front of my desk, looking more tired than I have seen her in a long while, and she stares at me intently.

"Mia, what is going on? You usually get lost in your work to a maddening degree, but rarely so much that you are here until the small hours of the night without keeping everyone on the team updated. You gave the team the location of the arms dealer hours ago, and the field team has been deployed. What the hell is going on? Talk to me."

Looking back down at my desk, I stare at the cut-out newspaper article and the MicroSD card... and, staring back at me from the newspaper article, my sister's smiling face. It was the last thing I would have expected to see. Both of the items came from the envelope O'Donnell had dropped off earlier in the day, not a prank he had prepared for me as I had thought.

I take a deep breath to try and steady myself and wrest the jumble of feelings back into submission before they can overwhelm me again.

"It's a newspaper clipping from *The Cedarwood Post* from 5 years ago about Lily's murder. It was wrapped around a MicroSD card in an origami style and stuffed in this envelope. Someone sent it to the office via messenger during the day, marked for my attention. I was working on tracking the arms dealer and almost forgot about it. I first thought it was another prank, as O'Donnell was the one who dropped it on my desk. And then, when I opened it... Seeing her face, Lily's face... I have no idea why anyone would send this to me and why now, all of a sudden, without cause. It's been years since her murder and even longer than that since I had left Cedarwood. I know I shouldn't react this badly to seeing her face and the article, but I can't help it. You know how things were for us."

I take another deep breath, the words pouring from me faster than I want them to as I look up at Angie again.

The shock on Angie's face at my words turns to contemplation as she looks back at me and then down at the piece of newspaper and the MicroSD card on my desk. I look down again, still in shock after uttering the words.

"I have no idea why this was sent to you, and I'm sorry that it's upset you. We'll check the security cameras tomorrow to see if we can trace who sent you the envelope but for now... Have you checked the MicroSD card yet, Mia?"

I peel my eyes away from Lily's smiling face, forever frozen at 19, and try to rein in the warring emotions that are again vying for first place to overwhelm me.

"No, I haven't. It took me a while to unfold the origami wrapping without tearing it. It was so intricate and beautiful that I didn't want to damage it. That should have already told me it wasn't O'Donnell. And you know I love puzzles. But when I saw Lily's face... It caught me off guard. I am actually not sure how long I have been sitting here, to be honest."

Angie's face softens, and her voice turns gentler. It turns into the voice that had comforted me when I had been handed over into FBI custody as a skinny and awkward fifteen-year-old, had helped me through my first heartbreak and the pain over my family's abandonment of me, and had looked after me when I had gotten sick and had no one else to take care of me.

"I think you need to take a look at that card before we do anything else."

I nod my agreement, already pulling my laptop closer to insert the MicroSD card into the reader as Angie walks around the desk to stand behind me.

A ping from my laptop shows the MicroSD card's content is ready to be viewed.

No password. No protection. It just opens. Strange.

The hacker in me is disappointed at the ease of access; the investigator in me wants to find answers immediately.

I click on the single folder showing on the card, and a simple set of files appears. These all seem more confusing than helpful at first glance. All are scanned newspaper articles about seemingly unrelated deaths and accidents, not only in Cedarwood but also in surrounding towns. All the files are named with the dates of the deaths they detail.

The exception is one scanned page: the last file in the folder. Whoever had set up the folder had named the last file "Muerte," which in itself is already strange, but stranger yet are the words written on the scanned page:

*They were not lucky in life*
*And these were no accidents*
*She confessed at the wrong time*
*And became collateral damage*
*The answers lie in death*

The words have been written on the original page in big block letters, as though the writer wanted to ensure that, no matter what, the words would scan well, but the scan makes them seem grotesque somehow—haunting, even.

I can feel Angie's brow furrow behind me in unison with my own as we stare at the articles opened on my laptop and the single newspaper clipping on my desk. I know she knows exactly what I am thinking. The curiosity and need for answers bubble up inside of me, winning out over my fears and doubts.

"You need to go back to Cedarwood, don't you?"

Putting in my leave is easy as I rarely take time off, and having the boss on your side never hurts. Angie also knows that I won't be able to let this rest, leave granted or not.

Heading home, I realize exactly how late it is as the streets are less crowded than normal, although still not quiet. This is the city that never sleeps, after all.

I quickly pack a bag, taking only a few minutes to throw some jeans, a few shirts, something warm, my running shoes, a pair of exercise shorts, and a T-shirt in a bag. I usually travel light. All I truly need is my laptop and phone, and I am ready to go. But this time, I need to make sure I have an outlet for anxiety, and a good run has never hurt me.

Looking down at myself, I realize my office shoes won't work well if any field work is required. Luckily, my favorite sneakers will do a great job, and I swap the heels for the sneakers. I am still not sure why I am required to dress somewhat formally at the office when I am much more comfortable and productive in jeans and sneakers.

Ready to go, I take a moment to look over my apartment. The tiny one-bedroom is where I have found peace and quiet (or as much quiet as you can get in New York) for my soul over the last two years, and I take a savoring breath. I am not sure how long I will be gone, but I know the Mia returning to this apartment won't be the same one leaving now.

The parking garage is eerily empty as I walk to my car, and a slight unease hits me about where I am about to go and who I might see. As a teenager, I had vowed never to return to Cedarwood, never to go back to the place where I had not felt loved or accepted. I am sure many remember me, not with kindness, and will feel that I shouldn't be welcomed or allowed into town.

But the need to find answers about my sister and to find out how these accidents relate to Lily outweighs the unease and the fear of what might await me.

Firming my resolve, I pop my bag and laptop onto the back seat, shift my car into drive, and hop onto the freeway towards Cedarwood—only 10 hours to go until I can start finding answers.

# Chapter 2:

I am not sure what exactly I was expecting, but it seems that little has changed in Cedarwood over the last 12 years. Driving into town at 10:00 in the morning, everything seems to be just as sleepy as I remember. A few suspicious looks are thrown my way, but that is how it has always been. Strangers are regarded with mistrust and doubt, and that is what I am now: a stranger to this town.

My parents had left Cedarwood a year or so after Lily's murder, Angie told me. Even if they had still been in town, I would not have stayed with them... not after all these years, and not even if it could help my investigation. There was too much hurt and too much unsaid.

I point the car in the direction of the only motel in town, but it is fully booked, leaving me with one option: the motel near the church. The motel is run by the church itself as a source of additional income for the church, and I am met by the church custodian, Adam, who handles the front desk.

The comic shock on his face when I give my name to book a room is almost enough to make me giggle. Adam had been the custodian of the church since I was in primary school, and I had dutifully greeted him every Sunday when attending church with my family.

Adam shows me to my room, lucky number 13, and I thank my lucky stars that I can take one of the single rooms. Sharing a room is not exactly conducive to a successful investigation when looking for murderers.

The room is bland but neat. A single bed, a small desk that doubles as the nightstand, and a lonely chair are the only furniture in the room. I have to share a bathroom with two other rooms, but as both are unoccupied at present, I have it all to myself.

I dump my bag in the room, not bothering to unpack for now, and prepare to head out by grabbing my laptop and the list of names I had printed out at the office before leaving. I know I should probably rest after driving all night, but the need to accomplish something, anything, right away keeps the tiredness at bay for the moment.

I know what I need to do first: get all the incident reports for the accidents as well as Lily's case. So I head to the one place where I will find all of this: the police station.

As I walk into the police station, my eyes need a moment to adjust to the somewhat dark interior. As my vision shifts, a handsome yet somewhat scruffy-looking man lifts his head to look at me from behind a desk. His dark eyes and brooding face pull me in, stopping me short for a moment. I plaster a smile on my face, trying to look friendly and open.

"Hi there. I'm hoping you can help me with some information today."

He puts down the pen he had been writing with and folds his hands on the desk in front of him.

"Detective Ethan Hayes. What do you need?"

His tone is not exactly the friendliest, but oh my, what a voice. Like silk hands running across my bare skin. I clear my throat, doing my best to keep a polite smile on my face, and ignore the slight thrill that ran through me just now. With those eyes and that voice...

Focus, Mia.

Clearing my throat, I say, "I was hoping you would be able to help me with files on a cold case and some accidents that had happened in Cedarwood over the last few years. I want to look at the more intimate details of the cases. The information I can find online and in the news is not exactly complete."

Detective Hayes' focus sharpens on my face, his eyes boring into mine as he tries to read behind my smile.

"I cannot give out files to someone walking in from the street." His tone is even less friendly now. "Unless you have a judge's order or you are here to take over a case, I suggest you make use of the information you can find online. If you are a journalist looking for a story, you are in the wrong town."

My heart sinks at his tone and the defensiveness of his words, almost like I had just insulted the town he lives in.

I sigh on the inside, knowing what I need to do and reveal. I really did not want to pull out my badge or state the reason I needed the files, but I guess I have to do that now. Angie and I decided that I should reveal as little as possible to make sure no one can impede my investigation, though not having the files will impede my investigation much more. Maybe Detective Gorgeous-but-Brooding can be of some help.

"Mia Conrad, FBI New York field office," I say in my official FBI agent voice as I hold up my badge for him to see, dropping my smile. His eyebrows flick up in surprise, those gorgeous and intense eyes sizing me up anew. "I received information at the FBI New York field office that there is more to Lily Conrad's case than previously thought and that it might be linked to some of the accidents that have occurred in Cedarwood and surrounding towns over the last few years. If you can then help me with the files, I would appreciate it, but I am happy to come back with a warrant if needed."

Detective Hayes' face turns thoughtful, and I see how a puzzle piece clicks into place for him.

"Hmm, I see. You are Lily's older sister; I see the resemblance now. You are the one that hacked the FBI and was then recruited by them as a teenager." I nod once, but his face reveals little of what else he is thinking, and I hold my breath as he pauses for much too long. "Give me the list of cases you want to look at, and I will pull the files for you."

Pleasantly surprised that he does not require further cajoling to give me the files, I walk around the front desk to him, pulling the printed list from my bag.

"I'm happy to wait for you to pull the files," I say, hoping that he will ask me to help. "I don't have anywhere else to be for the moment."

His eyes scan over the list, and he looks back up at me.

"Give me your number, I'll bring the files to you when I get off shift."

No "thank you, but no thank you," no acknowledgment of my offer to assist. I brush off my irritation at his lack of manners and the tiny tickle of irritation at the small part of myself that wanted to stay and help so that I could keep hearing that silken voice.

I pull out one of my official business cards and write my private cell phone number on the back. As I hand him the card, his fingers graze mine lightly. I am surprised to feel how soft and gentle his hands are, the complete opposite of his slightly scruffy-looking face with the stubble shining through definitely not what I had expected.

As I turn to leave the station, I can feel his eyes on my back. I know I am not bad to look at, and the jeans I am wearing hug my figure in all the right places. For a moment, just a moment, I wonder if he is enjoying the view.

I shake my head, trying to clear it. Exhaustion seems to be meddling with my thoughts and giving me strange ideas. I need to head back to the motel and catch up on some desperately needed sleep. Maybe the 10-hour trip took more out of me than I want to admit, and with 6 hours until Hayes gets off his shift, I have quite a bit of time to spare. As Angie likes to remind me: "Rest is also productive."

# Chapter 3:

On my way back to the motel to get some sleep, I stopped at the Raven Diner on Main Street to buy dinner, one of the few places I missed after moving to New York (although calling it 'moving' implies I had a choice in the matter). Miss Mary, the previous owner, was a kind woman and had always snuck me a piece of pie when I would come hide out here when things at home got too much. She was one of the few people who treated me with kindness and who seemed to understand that my home life was not as idyllic as my family made it out to be in public.

Waiting for my order, I look around the diner. Suddenly the ghosts of my parents coming in with Lily and myself appear in my mind's eye. They always sat us down in the booth closest to the street. Lily liked to watch people go by and wave at those she knew, jumping up regularly to greet a friend or a fellow student. She was everyone's favorite, a brilliant sun shining on the small shadow that I cast.

Turning my head away, I see the table where I used to hide from home life, playing on my laptop, figuring out coding on my own, and learning all I could from internet searches. The same table where Lily one day found me, realizing this is where I came to hide. After that, she would sometimes come and find me and bring friends with her to ridicule me for looking unfashionable and not fitting in. For being a weirdo.

My order number is called, and I try to shake the unwanted memories off as I walk over to collect the packaged meal. Thanking the young server, I hastily grab my meal and head to my car, back to the motel and away from the memories.

Lying on the bed in my motel room, I try to still my mind. It has been racing at about 1000 miles per hour ever since I received that envelope yesterday, and the ghosts that jumped out at me in the diner are not helping in any way. I desperately need to sleep right now, and

I had hoped my full stomach would aid in this, but no such luck. Being back here, in Cedarwood, so many memories that I have been repressing for years and years start to surface, unwanted and against my will as they had in the diner.

Fighting to keep the memories bottled up and locked away seems futile as a small headache starts to form above my eyes. The fight is pointless, though, and my mind is caught up in a storm that I cannot see a way out of. I have to go through it.

I knew that Lily was my parents' favorite; anyone could see that, and everyone in town understood. She was beautiful and kind to everyone except me and a few others she deemed too strange to merit her affection and kindness. Popular with teachers and kids alike, she was a petite girl with striking features who broke hearts wherever she went. I would not have cared, and she could have it all, had it not been for the fact that this, somehow, meant Lily was justified in her taunting and constant humiliation of me and who I was.

My mother's disapproving face, my father's disappointment in me, and Lily's justifications for taunting me come flooding into my mind in a cacophony of sounds and feelings as the memories pour through me in a torrent. But it is Lily's voice that stands out among them as it always did.

"Mia, you look terrible. You really need to find a fashion sense."

"Why can't you just put some makeup on? You look like a ghost."

"Ugh, just get some sun. You are pathetic, just typing away the whole day. What are you even doing?"

"You know that none of the boys like you, right? You know too much about computers. No wonder no one loves you."

"Why can't you just act normal? You keep embarrassing me at school! Everyone says you are weird."

"Mom, Mia is being mean to me, and I was only making a joke! She doesn't understand me."

"You are such a nerd. Why can't you just join the cheer squad or play a feminine sport like a normal girl?"

"Hiding out won't make you popular, Mia. You should honestly just get a life."

I remember. I remember every single detail of her face and voice as she spoke each horrid word to me. I can still feel the stares from my parents. In the beginning, I tried to stand up for myself, but that was quickly and brutally squashed by my mother as she scolded me.

"How dare you speak to your younger sister like that? Older sisters are supposed to protect their younger siblings, not hurt them! Apologize to Lily right now, and do not let me hear you speak to her like that again!"

My mother had given me a hiding and a half after these words, and I had been forced to apologize to Lily in front of my parents. They wanted to be sure I did it properly and that I had learned my lesson. The utter delight shining in Lily's eyes at this had broken something in me that day. That's when I knew for sure that I would need to look out for myself in life. There would be no kindness or love to be found in the structure my parents and sister called home. A foreign word to me for most of my life.

Until the day the FBI showed up at my parents' door.

I had hacked the FBI's main server on a dare from an older boy at school who had pretended to be kind to me. Something I had known very little of up to then.

The FBI had traced my hack, even though I thought I had been so clever in hiding my trail. But they found me due to my own arrogance, leaving my signature hidden in the code I had embedded on their server as an ode to myself and my brilliance.

Egotistical, that is what I had been.

My parents were obviously at first confused by the agents standing at their front door, not understanding what had happened to have led them there. Until then, Agent Angie West explained that this was in connection with their daughter and a hack she had pulled off.

As they called me down, the anger and disappointment radiated from them, stifling me until I could barely breathe.

But somehow, in the process of the FBI confiscating my laptop, agents packing up my room, and explaining to my parents what the options were, it all became about Lily.

Lily was embarrassed by her "criminal" older sister and immediately becomes hysterical.

Lily was crying because the neighbors were standing in the street, looking at our house, trying to figure out what was going on.

Lily was upset that she wouldn't ever be able to show her face in public again after the humiliation.

Lily was inconvenienced as she was unable to attend cheerleading practice due to the FBI's timing.

All the while, my parents barely listened as Agent West explained there were only two options for me: join the FBI or go to a detention facility. If I could hack the FBI from my crummy laptop without any formal training or assistance, they could not allow me to go about life unchecked, and they could not let a possible resource slip through their fingers like that either. Therefore, those were the only two choices they were offering.

During the discussion, not once did it register with Lily or my parents that I was the one who would be taken away from home and removed from all I know. They did not try to comfort me or fight for me as we sat in the living room, listening to Agent West explaining the options that the FBI was giving to my parents and me for my future.

I can understand that they weren't proud of what I had done, but knowing they did not care enough about me to worry about what would happen to me once I was taken away... That was too much to take in and process.

My parents were shocked, disappointed, disapproving, and enraged at my utter disregard for their feelings (as they put it) and signed me over to the FBI without a second thought, not caring which options the FBI decided to go with for my future. They were happy, I think, to be rid of me, and to no longer take responsibility for me, leaving them with just their darling Lily: the one who made them smile and brought only sunshine into their lives.

The last thing I remember as I was being taken away by the agents in a nondescript black car was that my parents were comforting Lily, assuring her that no one would think she had anything to do with this. Everyone knew she was a good and kind and decent person. My being taken away was for the best.

They had shut the front door before I had even gotten in the car.

No goodbye hugs or kisses.

No wishes for me or regrets about my actions spoken.

Not a single wave to send me off.

Just a closed front door and an empty porch.

Complete indifference.

Angie, seeing what I had grown up with and how I was treated, fought to make sure I was recruited to the cyber division of the New York field office as a hacker. She saw to my education and tried to be the family I never had. Perhaps because she, too, had no one else, we ended up being each other's family.

I tried to keep in touch with my parents and Lily, sending messages for birthdays and special days and check-ins, but I never received a reply from Lily. My parents would reply now and then, but requests to come home for the big holidays were declined as they would "not be good for Lily." For a full 6 years, I had heard absolutely nothing from them.

Until that phone call on my 21$^{st}$ birthday when happiness quickly turned to pain. Lily had gone missing three days earlier, and her body had been found the previous day. She had been strangled and left in the freezer at church.

My father's strained voice and my mother's crying in the background had been the last time I had heard from them. If it had not been for Angie updating me with information as she received it from the Cedarwood police station, I would have known absolutely nothing about my sister's case until the information was published in the newspapers.

Even though I was never close with Lily or my parents, knowing that I was not worth their time, even for birthdays and special occasions, or even to let me know if they found out what exactly had happened to my sister...

I do not want to admit it, but it hurt back then. And it still hurts today.

# Chapter 4:

I must have finally fallen asleep, as the ringing of my phone startles me awake. I had been having more flashbacks of my childhood in my nightmares, leaving me feeling clammy and confused.

I grab my phone, answering without checking the caller ID, and trying to keep the sleep and pain of the memories from my voice.

"Yes, hello. This is Mia."

Gods, can I sound more confused?

"It's Ethan Hayes. I'd like to bring the files over. I was able to pull the files from Cedarwood and the other towns."

Wow, he works quickly. I might just like that. And having that silky voice in my ear again... I could listen to him all day.

Dammit, Mia. Focus!

"Hi, Detective Hayes. That is great. Thank you for making quick work of the files. And yes, sure. I am staying at the motel in room 13."

"Call me Ethan. And I know where you are staying. I will see you in 10 minutes with the files."

The phone clicks off in my ear as I start replying to his arrangement. No goodbye or anything from his side. Well, I guess he is a man of action, not words.

Sitting up fully, I see my reflection in the mirror across the room and realize I desperately need to fix my hair and face before Ethan arrives. I look like I had been in a fight for my life, with my hair in complete disarray standing at odd angles around my head like some sort of crazy crown. I know I should have removed my mascara before I fell asleep, something I regularly forget, as I glare at the stripes and smudges across my face. Thank goodness I don't wear much else in the way of makeup, my face would have been scary as hell now.

Exactly 10 minutes later there is a single rap on my door, and I open to find Ethan standing there with a box full of files and two milkshakes from Raven Diner in hand.

"Hi, Ethan. Come in."

Smiling up at him, I am suddenly aware of exactly how tall he is, standing in the doorway. His hair is almost brushing the top of the door frame.

I open the door wider and move out of the way for him to enter.

"Let me move my laptop, and you can put the box down here."

I pick my laptop off the table and set it on the bed as Ethan makes his way to the table, putting the box and the milkshakes down and giving me a good look at his muscular back and shoulders.

He turns back towards me, and I shake my head ever so slightly, trying to move my focus to hearing what he is saying instead of, well... just looking at him.

"I brought you a milkshake as well. It helps me think, and I thought it might do the same for you."

I guess neither "hello" nor "goodbye" is something he bothers with. At least he comes bearing milkshakes. And his silky voice.

"Thanks, I appreciate it," I say as my attention shifts to the box of files on the table. The milkshake can wait, but those files... Those files could have the answers I need.

It takes me a moment, but the implication of his comment that he brought a milkshake for me "as well" sinks in, and I look over at him, seemingly waiting for me to comment.

Politely, I say, "Thank you for bringing the files and the milkshake. I will let you know as soon as I am done with the files."

Ethan turns his body to me in full, focusing his attention on me, his dark eyes locked onto my face. "I want to help," he says as his voice drops lower, becoming softer. "I didn't want to tell you this morning, but I was the one who discovered your sister's body that day. It was my first week on the job here and finding her in the freezer like that still haunts me. And the fact that we couldn't find her killer, that the trail seems to have gone cold... If there is a possibility of solving her murder, I want to be involved."

His face becomes more brooding at the last words, and he flicks his eyes down for a moment before looking up at me again. Gods, those eyes of his really are something. Mesmerizing.

I frown back at him and wonder about his revelation. As I draw a breath to reply, he cuts me off.

"One of the other names you gave, Natalie Keen," he continues, "I knew her as well. Grew up with her. She was a good person. If her death was not an accident, I want to help bring whoever ended her life to justice. Let me help, and I promise to see this through with you to find who is responsible for your sister's murder."

I close my mouth and cross my arms, trying to buy myself some time to think. Having a detective from the area helping me with the case could open doors and cut through a lot of red tape I do not have time for. Tape that I would otherwise have to circumvent with some of my more creative methods, which I know would be frowned upon by most people.

This is a massive gamble and could end badly for me, with the investigation leading to a dead end, or it could help the investigation move along more swiftly and save me time and energy.

Weighing the pros and cons and reaching a decision, I push down the creeping doubts and hold my hand out to Ethan. "Deal. As long as you don't get in my way and never lie to me or hide facts about any of the cases, no matter how bad or disturbing, I will be happy to have your assistance."

His eyes slowly slide down my face to my hand, feeling much too much like a caress, before he reaches for my hand, shaking it firmly.

"Where do you want to start?"

The partnership settled, Ethan takes a seat on the only chair in the room and grabs his milkshake and a random file from the top of the box. Knowing where I want to start and where I need to start, I look for Lily's file in the box.

Standing this close to him in my small room, I notice his smell for the first time. Deep and complex, yet easy on the nose. This is not helping my concentration or the feeling of him filling the room at all...

Clearing my thoughts, I grab my milkshake, mumble another "thank you" to Ethan, and plonk onto the bed, the only other seat in the room, my attention finally settling and focusing on the information in front of me.

Ethan clicks the light in the room on, and I become aware of my surroundings and my grumbling stomach as I blink at the suddenly bright light filling the space.

My legs are numb from sitting cross-legged, and I am sure my back will never recover from the hunched-over position I have been reading in. I get up gingerly, trying not to groan like I just turned 105, and look at the mess of files and notes all over the bed, table, and even on the floor that Ethan and I have made.

I try to stretch inconspicuously, giving Ethan a quick look to make sure he doesn't see, but he seems absorbed in the file in front of him, unaware of my cringing.

As I start going through the notes, trying to find links between the accidents, there is one thing that jumps out at me: all the accident victims were found to have had traces of either opioids, anti-anxiety medication, or illegal substances in their blood at the time of their accidents. None of the amounts were high enough to ring any alarm bells, and the county medical examiner had written this off as self-medication or drug abuse that led to impaired concentration, stating that this could have led to the accident that killed them.

That is, all except one. Natalie Keen, Ethan's friend. According to her toxicology report no substances were found in her system at the time of her death, and the medical examiner found that she had suffered a light heart attack that could have led to her losing concentration and driving off the road, fatally crashing into the boulder just off the shoulder of the road.

It seems the various investigating officers had agreed with the medical examiner on all the cases, as no foul play could be found at the accident scenes. Not with the vehicles, nor at the campsites where one person had fallen to their death, and another had been hit by a falling boulder, nor with the hiker who had slipped and fallen down a slope, hitting her head on a broken tree trunk on the way down.

With the deaths all being written off as accidents, there was no reason to link them to Lily except for the drugs that had been found in some of the accident victim's bodies. Lily had been brutally strangled and her body stashed in the freezer at the church, and she had heroin in her system at the time of her death. It was a drug she had never used, according to the statements from my parents and her friends. She was a happy, good girl who did not do drugs.

Shaking my head at my parents' ignorance of what teenagers and young adults are capable of, I start to arrange the cases in date order, trying to find other patterns or similarities between the cases, anything that could be a link or a whiff of a link.

Slowly, very slowly, a pattern emerges between the cases, although I doubt my own eyes. Grabbing the map of the county Ethan had in the box, I mark the locations of the accidents on the map, adding the date of the accident to each marking to keep track of who the victim was.

All the accidents happened almost as far as possible from one another, as though someone had planned it out to ensure the accidents and the toxicology similarities could not be linked. As they were all spaced 6 to 8 months apart, it would have made it difficult for anyone to draw any conclusions about similarities.

I still have no idea how this connects to Lily's murder, but the toxicology link is scratching at me. There has to be more there. If only Natalie Keen's toxicology made sense and linked to the rest.

Staring down at the map on the floor, trying to figure out what I might be missing, I almost hit Ethan in the face when he suddenly speaks next to me. "I think you might have found something promising here."

When did he get up from the chair and kneel on the floor next to me? And why does it seem that men like to give me a fright when I am concentrating? And why, oh why, does he need to smell so good?

Trying my best to keep the irritation at the fright and my momentary lapse in concentration from my voice, I ask the question that has been bugging me about the one missing link: Natalie Keen.

"The accidents and the pattern in which they occurred make sense when seen as a whole, but the fact that Natalie Keen had no drugs or any other substances in her system is bothering me. How does she link in with the rest if she didn't have any substances in her system? Do you think the medical examiner could have made a mistake with her toxicology report? She was so young; it seems highly unlikely that a heart attack could have been the cause of death."

Turning my head to Ethan, I see him rock back on his heels, his face becoming guarded and those brooding eyes fixing on the map.

The creeping suspicion that he is hiding something makes me press harder.

"You said you knew her. Do you know anything about her medical history or family history? Does her family have a history of heart attacks or heart disease?"

I can feel Ethan's discomfort at my questions as he straightens up, looking at the files on the desk.

"I do not know her family well enough to comment on the heart disease, but Natalie was healthy as far as I know."

My feeling that Ethan is done with the conversation is confirmed as he turns back to me, a slight smile on his face.

"That is the fourth time your stomach has growled in the last ten minutes. Perhaps we should take a break and find something to eat. It's Thursday, so there is a two-for-one burger special at the Raven Diner. If you'd like to join me."

I nod my agreement, fighting against the slight blush coloring my cheeks. I didn't realize he could hear my stomach growling, and now that it has been mentioned, my stomach seems adamant about doing a whole opera for us.

Pushing myself off the floor to grab my shoes and bag, I vow to myself that I will get the answers about Natalie Keen from Ethan. One way or another.

He might be stubborn, but he doesn't know me very well yet.

I am stubborn as hell, and I do not give up.

Ever.

# Chapter 5:

The burgers are as good as I remember, but the stares Ethan and I are getting from other people in the diner have me wishing we had gotten the food to go.

A few people who recognize me quickly look away when they see me looking back at them. The only person who dares to come and greet me like a normal human being is Miss Scheckter, my middle school math teacher, but she never cared what anyone thought of her. By Cedarwood standards, she's a crazy spinster who spends too much time with her cats. To me, she's one of the few sane people here.

People seem to somewhat ignore Ethan as well, politely nodding at the detective but not sticking around to make small talk with him.

Eating my chips slowly, enjoying the companionable silence at our table, and sifting through all the details we've uncovered, an idea suddenly pops into my head.

"You know, some of the drugs that were found in the victims' systems need a prescription for dispensing, like Valium. We should find out if any of them had prescriptions for the drugs and track who else in town uses the same type of drug. I didn't see any notes about this in their files, only the statements from family and friends who had been interviewed. We would need to speak to all the doctors in the towns where the victims lived, but it could be an important link and help to rule out accidental death completely. I mean, they could have been drugged against their will."

Ethan slowly puts down the burger he was biting into and swallows, my eyes following the slight bob of his throat and his tongue as he licks a bit of sauce from his lips.

"You're right. We need to speak to a doctor, and I know who we can start with. Kyle Reynolds is the current town physician and will be the best bet, as his father is one of the deaths on your list."

"Wait. Kyle Reynolds? The Kyle Reynolds?"

I struggle to keep the surprise from my face as I process this bit of news. When did the local bad boy have time to become a doctor? As far as I can remember, he never excelled at anything other than football and hooking up with every single girl who smiled his way.

Knowing I am failing terribly at hiding my surprise, I look down at my plate to grab a chip and shove it in my mouth. Hopefully, the perfectly crunchy bit of potato can distract me enough to normalize the look on my face. As I bring the chip to my mouth, I notice Ethan staring intently at my mouth. This second surprise in as many minutes has me forgetting how to eat, putting the chip down hastily, and averting my eyes.

I look back up to see Ethan picking up his burger and continuing his meal as though nothing had happened. Did I just imagine that, or am I losing my mind?

As Ethan takes the last bite of his burger, he signals for the server to bring our bill, and I relax a bit in relief.

Focus, Mia.

There can be no distractions over the next few days and weeks, or however long it takes me to solve this case.

Focus.

Ethan and I arrange to meet at Kyle's office at 8:00 am so that we can get in to see him before he is swamped with patients.

Sitting in the waiting room with Ethan, incredibly aware of his warmth next to me, I look around, hoping to have my attention snagged by something else.

My relief when Kyle's assistant waves us through feels utterly childish to me, as Ethan once again seems not even to notice I am there. I am imagining things, or is the brooding detective just skilled at hiding his feelings?

Walking into Kyle's office feels strange as I would never have associated him with a career that performs any type of service, except perhaps a stripper. He is just as gorgeous as I remember from school.

The boyish smile, the half dimples, the perfect teeth, the well-maintained body, and the perfect hair all look the same as he comes around his desk to greet us. The only difference is that he swapped the football jersey for a white coat.

"Mia Conrad! I didn't believe my assistant when she gave me your name, but here you are. You look great! How are you?"

He grabs me into a bear hug, leaving me at a total loss for words. Here was a jock who had no idea I even existed in high school, giving me a welcome and a half. Flabbergasted is not even the word.

"And Ethan, how are you?"

Kyle shakes Ethan's hand, and I see the slight look they give each other like two boxers sizing each other up before a match. Except today, there would be no match. I need answers, and a bit of male ego will not stand in my way.

"Hi, Kyle. It's good to see you. I was surprised to hear you are the town doctor, but I'm glad that you are well," I interject before the sizing up can continue. "How are your mom and sister doing?"

Kyle immediately and enthusiastically launches into a tale of his family and their lives as he takes a seat behind his desk again, motioning for us to sit down in front of the desk.

I politely wait for Kyle to finish his story before I say anything or bring up the reason for our visit. I can feel Ethan's impatience at Kyle's story growing beside me, but I wave a hand at him not to say anything. We need to be careful not to piss Kyle off and lose his assistance. It would take a lot to convince a judge to give us a warrant for medical records when we do not have a case (yet), and I do not fancy the prospect of breaking and entering to temporarily borrow the files without permission and then having to break in again to return said files. Too much noise and too much that can go wrong.

As Kyle finishes his story, I try to think of the way to best ask for his assistance. He catches me a bit off guard as he says, "I am sure you are not here just to hear how my family members are getting on with life and to catch up, though I am sure you have some fantastic stories to share from your work for the FBI. How can I help a federal agent and our town's detective?"

His smirk at the last words has Ethan tensing up. Not that I blame him, but this was the Kyle I knew. The bad boy who liked to be in charge and liked it when kids would come to him to fawn over him and try and be his friend. The bad boy who made all the girls, and a few of the moms, swoon.

I lightly clear my throat, choosing my words carefully.

"Kyle, I received information about Lily's murder and a string of accidents that occurred in Cedarwood as well as surrounding towns over the last few years. One of the accidents is your father's. I believe that these accidents might have been caused intentionally, making them murders. And we need your assistance to find some of the information regarding not only the victims but also a few other people in Cedarwood and the other towns."

I put the list of names down in front of Kyle on his desk, and his face turns pensive as he leans forward in his chair, staring at the list.

"I understand that this is a lot to take in," I continue, "and if you are unable to help, I get it. But we need to look into the medical records of the accident victims as well as find out who has prescriptions for certain specific drugs in town. This will significantly speed up our investigation and help us rule out accidental death more convincingly."

Ethan shifts in his seat next to me but remains quiet, allowing me to do the talking and to convince Kyle to assist us.

"One of the drugs that was found was Valium, and I know that can only be dispensed to someone with a prescription, not over the counter. If we could trace who might have been dispensed Valium in the period relating to the specific accidents where it was found in the victim's system, it could lead us to a breakthrough in the case or at least give us a connection in the case. I know it feels unethical to pull the records of patients who are still alive, but this information could help solve the case and perhaps save lives. I'm sure there are more of these so-called accidents to come."

I hadn't previously voiced my suspicions about another accident occurring to Ethan but going by the timeline I had plotted last night, an "accident" was due soon with the last one happening six months ago. Still, he says nothing, seemingly fixing his entire attention on Kyle. A small bit of disappointment goes through me at this. He could at least acknowledge my words and suspicion with a nod, but I shake off the tiny disappointment as I wait for Kyle's reply.

"I can look into who in town has a prescription for Valium or any of the other opioids that were found," Kyle says to my surprise after a few moments of silence. "But I can almost guarantee it will be a dead end. Mental health is still frowned upon by many in small towns and rather treated with a steady regime of denial instead of professional help and drugs."

I sneak a look at Ethan to see his reaction to this information, but his face is a mask of contemplation. I turn my attention back to Kyle.

"Thank you, Kyle. I appreciate you offering the assistance; it will cut through a lot of red tape. I know it might not yield results or the results we want, but I appreciate you getting the information for us in any way. I'd rather have too much information than none."

Ready to leave, Ethan and I start getting up, but Kyle stops us with a hand gesture.

"Look, I know the doctors from the other towns won't help you, not by a long shot, but I can pull the records for all the victims if you can give me a day or two. The county shares a medical system, and I can put a request in for the information. It might just take a bit of time."

"Thank you, Kyle," Ethan calmly says, getting the jump on me. "That would be of great help."

The three of us get up, Kyle and Ethan shaking hands. As Kyle turns to me, taking my hand, his face becomes more serious.

"If you need help speaking to any of the families or friends, let me know. I know everyone in town, and if someone is killing people in my home, I want to do what I can to stop them. I honestly never believed my father lost control of his truck that day, and I'm glad you are looking into this. I'll give you all the help you need, no questions asked."

I blink in surprise at his earnest words and the honesty on his face. Kyle might be the town's bad boy, but beneath it all, there is a good heart and what I hope to be pure intentions.

An unlikely ally for our team, but just perhaps the one we need.

As Ethan and I walk out of Kyle's office, I can feel Ethan building up to say something, and I let the silence between us hang to give him a chance to gather his thoughts.

We walk to our cars in the same pregnant silence, Ethan seeming to need the time to put his words in the right order.

"Mia..."

I stop at my car, looking over my shoulder and back at Ethan where he's stopped by the back of my car. His face is even more brooding than usual, his brow furrowed.

"Yes?"

"I know I suggested Kyle as the person to assist us with the information, and that was the right call to make, but I think you should be careful with him. I know it is none of my business. He was just much too..."

Words seem to fail Ethan as he scowls at me, seemingly hoping that I can read his mind.

I look up at him, utterly puzzled, trying to decipher his words and his sudden mood change.

"I can look after myself if that is what you are worried about. I did have basic field training before I became an official FBI agent, you know. And I enjoy the occasional Muay Thai class," I say, the meaning of his words dawning on me. "Besides, there is no way Kyle would look twice at me. I might be easy on the eyes, but I know I am no beauty.

And his type is only concerned with the exterior or what they can get from anyone. I know from experience."

I grimace at the last bit of the sentence, remembering how I had learned this the hard way about Kyle and his friends all those years ago right here in Cedarwood.

As I open my car door, Ethan is suddenly right next to me, his hand keeping me from opening the door and getting in. His intoxicating smell and warmth blanket my unease at the memories as I look up at him, into those magnetic eyes.

"Don't underestimate yourself, Mia," Ethan breathes, his voice low and sensual, like silk-gloved hands trailing across my skin, leaving me hot and cold all at once. His eyes are captivating and inescapable as he stares down at me. "You have a beauty that can make any man fall for you, whether he wants to or not. And adding in your intellect and charm... You are a lethal combination, Mia. Never forget that. I will call you later today so that we can go through the rest of the details of the files."

As Ethan turns around and walks to his car, again without a goodbye, the blood rushes to my face, and I feel my knees threaten to give out from under me.

I yank open my car door, practically falling into the front seat. Did that just happen, or am I imagining things?

It's too hot for a run but not for coffee. I need coffee. And to talk to Angie.

I turn my car on and head to one of the few new places in town, Aroma Café. Hopefully, they have bottomless coffee and good cake so that I can work through the fractured thoughts in my head.

# **Chapter 6:**

The coffee and cake were good, and it helped to nullify some of the irritation from parting my conversation with Ethan. What helped most, in the end, was the phone call with Angie. I had updated her on what we found as well as the note that was on my door.

Angie's last words to me before she had to rush off are still milling about in my head as I head back to the motel.

"Be careful, Mia. You do not know much about this detective, and anyone willing to threaten an FBI agent does not care if they get their hands dirty."

It is true; I do not know Ethan. And the threat posted on my door definitely points to someone who would play dirty. Could Ethan be that someone?

I sigh as I walk into the motel room, dropping my laptop bag on the bed. The table is still occupied with all the files and notes from yesterday, as well as the map. Even the chair is stacked with notes.

I plop onto the bed, my stomach full of the coffee and cake and the details I had shared with Angie playing in my mind.

There must be other similarities, other clues hidden in the files, things that we missed going through the files last night. I need to look them over again with fresh eyes.

I reach for the top file, but my eye catches my laptop bag. That MicroSD card that was sent to me... I had only looked at it once thus far in my shock at the information and the haste to get to Cedarwood. Perhaps there is something I missed, more information than could be seen on the surface.

It still bothered me that there were no passwords or other protections on the card. Why would someone make it that easy for me to find the information?

There may be something hiding beneath the surface.

I grab my laptop, determined to find more on the card. I open all the files and start checking every single detail, and there, right there, is something strange in the file size of the scanned page with the name "Muerte." The file is larger than it should be. Not astronomically, but enough to make me look twice.

Working my magic, I dig deeper and uncover a single link and a photo of another scanned page. I recognize the link as one of the dark web notice sites that I sometimes scour for details on cases (it is crazy what some murderers are willing to post to ensure their work has an audience and they get recognition for their "brilliance"). The scanned page is, again, a written page, written in those large letters.

*Follow the link*
*Find the answers and the Key*
*Time is not on your side*

Ominous, but it also confirms my suspicion that another "accident" is imminent. I have to solve this. And fast.

I turn my attention to the link and follow it to a single noticeboard on the notice site. The noticeboard is owned by a user with the online name MasterOfAll and no other details are visible, which is not uncommon for the dark web. Here your identity is not a secret by choice but due to necessity.

The noticeboard is empty, but perhaps with a bit of digging, I can find his IP address or the noticeboard's history.

Three hours later, I have all the messages posted on the noticeboard since it was created. MasterOfAll might be able to hide their IP address and true identity from me for the moment, but not the messages they posted.

The messages all have the same structure and were posted in 6-to-8-month intervals, the same frequency at which the accidents had happened. This is something, something big. I can feel it.

I read through the messages, and none of them make sense. They look more like random numbers that are repeated for each person than anything else. But they all start off with the words "Día de los Muertos" in the first line, or "Day of the Dead." The second line of each message is even more confusing: "Repent, and your sins will be forgiven."

As far as I could gather from the files last night, none of the victims have ever visited Mexico or been outside of the States, for that matter. None of them were overly religious, even though some of them attended church. What would they need to repent for? Most of them were beloved members of the community, according to the witness statements.

I open a blank document on my laptop and make a list of the dates of the messages and to whom they were sent.

Each person received only two messages: one message exactly two weeks and two days before their accident, and another message two days before they died. The messages sent to each person are exactly the same, which makes it even more confusing.

Now that the date pattern makes sense, I go back to the first message trying to find a pattern or details that I can use to decipher the message.

*Día de los Muertos*
*Repent, and your sins will be forgiven*
*43 9 15 91 3*
*90 14 112 35*
*20 50 72 18*
*101 11 85 44*
*61 1 164*

My knowledge of where the Day of the Dead is concerned is minimal, but a quick internet search tells me that it is a holiday widely celebrated in Mexico on the first and second of November each year. Depending on the location, the holiday is also celebrated on other days in October and November.

Okay, so I have the dates of the messages that correlate to the accidents and a Mexican holiday that celebrates and pays respect to the departed. How do these come together, and where does the repenting fit in?

For a moment, I shelve my thoughts of trying to tie all of this together and focus on the numbers.

I scrap the idea of coordinates immediately, as that does not make sense here at all. Phone numbers? No. Addresses? None of that makes sense. Postal codes or zip codes? Also no.

Running through the different options in my mind and coming up with nothing else for the moment, I scan my eyes over the second message that was sent to the first person. The opening lines of the second message differ slightly from the first message, and the numbers are different. I skip to the second message sent to the second person and the third person. They are identical to what the first victim received.

Frowning, I read through the message again.

*Día de los Muertos*

*Forgiveness is yours to receive*

*7 67 109*

*95 10 87*

*31 77 12*

Whatever the first message had conveyed to each of the victims, it seems that by following the details or instructions, they were promised forgiveness.

I lean back from my laptop, shaking my head. What on earth could any of the victims have done that they would get caught up in something that ended their lives…?

Letting my mind wander for a bit, thinking of the victims, the messages, and the similarities and differences between them, it strikes me that they all received the same messages and would have needed a way to decipher them.

My mind snaps back to the scanned page that was hidden. I pull it up again and look more closely. Yes, the word "key" is written with a capital letter even though it is at the end of a sentence. None of the other scanned pages have this. This has to be another clue, something the messenger wanted me to find and use.

If all the victims needed to decipher the exact same messages, they would have needed to use a key. The same key!

The reference to the Day of the Dead suddenly clicks into place: it isn't a reference to the actual holiday, but the key that all the victims had to use to understand the messages.

The realization hitting me is thrilling relief, the taste of the hunt, of solving the puzzle.

Now to find out if the reference is to a book, a website, or something else altogether.

A few hours later, my research is interrupted by a message from Ethan letting me know he is on his way.

Looking up from my phone screen to my laptop screen, I contemplate the messages and my findings. I know I told Ethan I value honesty above all and that he should not lie to me while we are working on this, but I am not sure how much I can share with him. I still feel as though there is something about Natalie Keen that he is hiding from me.

The knock on my door breaks my train of thought. I get up to open it and find Ethan holding coffee and a brown paper bag.

"No knife in your door today, I see," he says as a way of greeting.

"I guess whoever it was is giving me some time to pack, or they realized I can't be scared away," I say, shrugging.

Ethan doesn't comment on my reply, rather continuing into the room and putting the coffee and bag on the table next to my laptop. Is this man determined to feed me, or does he just enjoy showing up with beverages and food wherever he goes? Not that I'm going to complain. This morning's coffee and cake are a distant memory by now.

Sitting down on the only chair, Ethan turns to me, handing me a coffee.

"Were you able to find anything further in the files yet?"

I reach for the coffee. Staring down at it, I run through my earlier thoughts. I look back up at him, the brooding face and the intense eyes, hoping to see something there that can give me all the answers I am looking for.

I took a leap of faith, agreeing to work with Ethan on this case. Turning back now would be a waste of time.

"I haven't gone through the files again. I looked at the MicroSD card again and found a file and a website link embedded in the scan named 'Meurte,' hidden away. Let me show you."

Moving to sit on the bed, I pull my laptop closer and open the files in the order I had discovered them. Ethan moves the chair next to the bed, leaning over to see the laptop screen.

It's been a few minutes since I finished explaining to Ethan what I found, but silence has been his only answer thus far. He asked no questions while I showed him what I had found, only commented agreement on my thoughts as to what the numbers could not be. No comment on what they might be.

Still silent, Ethan reaches out and pulls the paper bag closer, handing me a croissant.

I take a bite, and oh my, it is heaven. Sweet, but not too sweet. Buttery and flaky on the outside and soft on the inside, filled with something that tastes like almonds. I am more than happy to wait for Ethan to process the information while I am enjoying this bit of deliciousness.

Clearing his throat, Ethan turns his frowning face to me.

"I cannot remember seeing anything in the files that tie in with Mexico or the Day of the Dead. I think we might need to interview family and friends of the victims to see if they can shed any light on this. The key will be virtually impossible to find without assistance to narrow down the search parameters."

I nod my agreement past my mouthful of croissant and swallow the last of the delicious treat.

"I agree, although I am not sure if any of the victims will have told their families anything worthwhile. We might need to dig deeper into their private lives for anything they could have kept hidden. Perhaps we can start with Kyle's mom; he did offer to help where possible, and I think she will be more inclined to speak to us if he is there as well."

Ethan starts nodding, opening his mouth to answer me, but the ringing of his phone interrupts the thought.

"Detective Hayes. Yes. I see. No, I will come through. Just send the coordinates to my phone."

Again, no formal greeting to end the call. I really need to ask him about that. For the moment, though, I decide to play nice. Personal feelings regarding manners can be left aside for a while longer.

"I need to go. A barn was burnt down on the Richards' farm last night from what seems to be a bonfire party, and their truck is missing, along with two sheep," he says as he sighs heavily. "Probably a bunch of teenagers gone wild, but I need to go out and make sure there's nothing more to it."

"I'll call Kyle in the meantime and set up an interview with his mom. I'll keep you updated if I find anything."

As Ethan gets up, I grab my phone to dial Kyle's number, hoping that I can speak to his mom today. The phone ringing in my ear is interrupted by Ethan looking back at me from the door, his brooding eyes looking me over.

"Be careful with your questions, Mia. I know you know how to do your job and handle yourself, but we don't want to spook anyone in town."

Before I can reply, Kyle answers on the other end of the phone, and Ethan closes the motel room door behind him, brushing off my anger at his comment.

Focus now, and deal with the anger later.

Focus, Mia.

# Chapter 7:

Kyle seemed happy to assist me in arranging a meeting with his mom and invited me over to her house for afternoon tea.

Seeing as I have an hour to kill before I need to be at Mrs. Reynolds' house, I rummage through my laptop bag in search of sticky tape or something that I can use to put notes up on the closet doors. As much as I love my laptop, which is the most stable thing in my life besides Angie, sometimes it is easier to visualize the whole picture and make connections when you can see all the information in front of you, not just on a screen.

My abysmal unpacking skills are finally working in my favor, I have Scotch tape in my backpack from who the hell knows how long ago, and I start putting up the victim's photos and names onto the closet doors, along with Lily's details.

The two messages each of these people received I put in the middle of the photos with a note beneath that reads "Key?".

Writing down the cause of death per person, I add this to each photo and stand back to look at my makeshift board, trying to fit the pieces of the puzzle together.

Somehow, all these people ended up receiving the exact same message, with their deaths following a similar pattern and timeline even though they did not die in the same manner. How? And what led them to receive these messages in the first place?

My phone pings, and I realize I only have 15 minutes to clean myself up a bit and get to Mrs. Reynolds.

I quickly drag a brush through my hair, touch up my mascara, and grab my laptop bag and keys.

Walking to my car, I go through the questions I need to ask Mrs. Reynolds while I try not to think about the comments or questions I might have to face. Hopefully, she is as kind, sweet, and proper as

I remember her to be, and there will not be any questions for me to answer.

I stop in front of my car. Something doesn't look right; the car seems to be leaning to the passenger side. As I walk around, I see why: a knife is stuck in the front wheel right next to a long slash in the tire. The knife has been left there as a message. It's the same type of knife that had been used to nail the message to my door.

This cannot simply be about me being back in Cedarwood. Someone wants me gone. Someone wants me to stop investigating this case.

My frown turns into a grimace of determination.

I am not one to run away, and if they—whoever they may be—find it out the hard way, then so be it. Threats be damned.

I throw my laptop bag and jacket into the car, popping the trunk.

Time to change a tire.

I arrive at Mrs. Reynolds' house a few minutes late, and a slashed tire in the trunk of my car. As I pull into the driveway, Kyle comes out of the front door.

"Hey, Mia. Good to see you again!" he calls from a distance, smiling, as I get out of my car.

"Hey, Kyle. Good to see you, too. Thank you for helping to set up this meeting with your mom."

I shoulder my laptop bag, leave my jacket in the car, and walk up to the porch where Kyle is waiting.

"Is that Mia, honey? Invite her in!"

Mrs. Reynolds' voice from inside the house is as kind as I remember it, and Kyle ushers me in, directing me to the living room.

"How are you, my dear? Come, sit. Sit!"

Everything looks almost exactly like I remember it, except that there are now more photos on the walls.

Sitting down, I politely make small talk for a while, hoping to find a gap to ask the questions I need to. Luckily, Kyle comes to my aid when he interrupts his mom in the middle of her tale about the garden renovations that she started after Mr. Reynolds' passing.

"Mom, Mia is not here to catch up. She needs to ask you a few questions about Dad if that's okay. There is a possibility that Dad's accident wasn't an accident after all, as I suspected. Please hear her out and answer any questions she has. If it wasn't an accident, we need to find whoever did this to Dad and our family."

Mrs. Reynolds goes quiet, and her face drains of color as Kyle speaks. I feel a prick of guilt for having to ask questions of someone who is still grieving her husband. But this needs to be done.

"What Kyle says is true, Mrs. Reynolds," I say gently. "I am sorry to have to open old wounds. But figuring out what happened to your husband could help me solve Lily's murder. As you know, there has been no arrest made in connection with her murder, and there are no further clues. I might not have been here during the last years of Lily's life, but she was still my family. I still want to solve her murder and get justice for her and any other victims that there might be."

I can feel the shock from Mrs. Reynolds as I bring up my sister's murder in the same breath as her husband's death and feel that prick of guilt again.

"I know this is all overwhelming and sudden, but if you allow me to ask you a few questions, I promise I won't bother you again about any of this. I just want to find answers, and I am sure you do too."

Mrs. Reynolds silently rearranges her facial expression into a calm look and clears her throat. The speed at which she can do it surprises me. It is almost as though she is used to hiding her feelings as if she has had years of practice. I ponder this for a moment before she interrupts my train of thought.

"Can I pour you coffee or tea? I find a good cup of coffee or tea can make any conversation easier."

At this, she moves forward on the couch to the refreshments laid out on the coffee table, waiting for a reply.

I swallow my thoughts and surprise, indicating that I would like coffee. Kyle also takes a cup of coffee, and Mrs. Reynolds pours herself tea before settling back on the couch.

"Well, Mia, dear. Ask me your questions, and let's see if I can assist in any way. I know how your parents grieved after your sister's death, and I do not wish it upon any parent to lose a child. If there is a way that I can help, I will do what I can, but I am honestly not sure what my Bob could have to do with it. The police ruled his accident as purely that: an accident."

I take a moment to gather my thoughts while looking down at my coffee in the lovely porcelain cup.

"Mrs. Reynolds, the medical report for Mr. Reynolds stated that he had drugs in his system, anti-anxiety medication, which caused him to lose focus, and that was ruled the cause of the accident. Was Mr. Reynolds on any such medications at the time of his death? Or were you aware that he was taking any similar drugs, perhaps?"

"No, Bob never took medication. He hardly ever took pain tablets, not even when he broke his clavicle. Like I told the police when they asked me the same question: Bob was much too stubborn even to admit when he felt anxious. He would definitely not have taken any drugs for it."

Out of the corner of my eye, I see Kyle nodding at his mom's words, agreeing. Making a note of her reply, I press on, knowing the next few questions might not be as easy for Mrs. Reynolds to answer.

"In the two to three weeks before Mr. Reynolds' death, did he do anything out of the ordinary or behave differently? Did he go on any road trips or disappear for a time? Any small detail that you can remember can be helpful."

At this, Mrs. Reynolds stiffens somewhat, giving Kyle a subtle sideways glance as though she wants to see his reaction to the question. Or perhaps she cannot reply to the question honestly in front of him.

She tries to hide her discomfort by taking a sip of her tea before she answers me, but I have already seen and noted her reaction. I wonder what the cause can be.

"In those last three weeks, Bob did not do much out of the ordinary, but he did go on a trip. He said he was going fishing one day, I think it was a Thursday, but when he got home, there was no fish, his gear was clean, and he was incredibly tired like he had been driving for long." I see her glance quickly at Kyle before continuing. "I... I didn't know what to think, so... So, the next morning, on my way to the shops, I made sure to take the truck instead of my car, and the mileage did not make sense. The dam is only twenty-five miles away, but his truck had done over a thousand miles in one day. I usually do not take note of such things, but I had driven his truck the Wednesday when I had to pick up a tree from the nursery. Remember, Kyle, it's that big sycamore you helped me plant in the back."

Looking down at her cup, Mrs. Reynolds pauses. When she continues, her voice is a bit softer and sadder.

"After that, he was a bit jumpy for a few days, but I didn't want to question him. It didn't feel worth the fight to ask him where he had been, and he was being so kind and gentle at that time. And, perhaps, I did not want to know the truth, especially if there was another woman."

"Mom, you can't really believe Dad would have cheated on you! He loved you," Kyle interjects, shocked at his mom's confession.

"Kyle, your mom has every right to think what she thinks. There is no judgment here," I say as I turn to face him before shifting my attention back to his mom. "Mrs. Reynolds, I can understand why you would think that, and thank you for sharing your suspicions. Is there anything else that stood out to you?"

Flicking a glance at a now-sullen Kyle, Mrs. Reynolds looks back up at me.

"The only other odd thing at that time was that Bob was quite attached to his phone, and I caught him reading an online paper on holidays in Mexico. He got a huge fright when he saw that I was behind him and immediately stormed off, quite angry. I thought it might have been because he was planning a holiday to Mexico for us. I have always wanted to go but have never had the chance."

The last words came out even softer, but my focus immediately zooms in on the online paper about Mexico. Could this be the key that I am looking for? I would need to find the paper and then check if any of the other victims had read the same thing.

"Mrs. Reynolds, can you remember what the paper was called, the one about Mexico that Mr. Reynolds was reading?"

Looking flabbergasted at my question, Mrs. Reynolds shakes her head.

"No, dear, I cannot remember. I only briefly saw a few words that stood out, and that was Mexico and holidays. Nothing else, unfortunately."

I take a moment to process the information, realizing that I will need to get into Mr. Reynolds' browser history to extract the relAngiet URL.

"Do you still have Mr. Reynolds' phone? It would help me if I could view the paper."

Without a word, Mrs. Reynolds gets up, goes straight to a drawer in the porcelain cabinet, and pulls out an old phone with its charger.

"If it will help you, please take it," Mrs. Reynolds says as she hands me the phone. "I have no use for it but have felt too heartbroken to get rid of it. The pin for the phone is Kyle's birthday, 04 16 98."

Kyle looks up at the mention of his birth date as the code, sadness on his face, but the sullenness of his mom's allegation that she thought his dad had cheated still lingers on his face.

As I thank Mrs. Reynolds for the phone and her answers and bid her farewell, I get up, grab my laptop bag, and start walking towards the front door. Better to get out now before there are any family discussions that I do not want to be part of.

Kyle greets his mom and jumps up to stop me just outside the front door.

"Mia, will you join me for a drink? Please."

I really want to get into the phone and start looking, but the pleading tone of Kyle's voice and the look on his face have me agreeing against my better judgment. I can also do with a beer or two.

Sitting in Lucky Star, one of the nicer bars in town, Kyle peppers me with questions about my time in the FBI and what had happened to me since I was taken to New York.

I try to give as little information as possible without being mean about it, but Kyle is so charming and disarming that I find myself sharing more than I planned to share with anyone in this town.

As the beer keeps flowing, I realize that I am enjoying this time with Kyle, and I want to ask him about his life as well.

But when I ask him about all the girls he dated in school, he laughs.

"Yeah, I was a real dickhead in school. Okay, well, after school as well. My ego and the popular thing went to my head," he admits before he takes another sip of his beer. "You know, I only started thinking of serious relationships after Lily and I had been dating for a few months."

The shock on my face brings him up short, coloring his cheeks with a blush.

"You and Lily dated? Why didn't you mention this before?"

"To be honest, I didn't know how you would react. But I guess the beer makes it easier for me to talk, so I'm hoping it makes it easier for you to listen."

I swallow my surprise, asking, "For how long did the two of you date?"

"We dated for about nine months, but she broke up with me the morning before she was murdered. It was brutal, losing her twice. At that point, I had thought she would be the woman that I married and settled down with. Had kids with."

This man is full of surprises.

I get up to get us another round of beers, still chewing on his revelation about Lily. I wonder if he could tell me more about her and the last few weeks before her murder. Perhaps I can use his inebriation to my advantage here to get some answers from him.

As I return to the table, I put Kyle's beer down in front of him, taking a sip of my own.

"Tell me about your relationship with Lily."

I am furious. No, that is not even the word for this emotion. I am beyond furious as I storm into the motel room.

Lily was incredibly religious, and Kyle... Kyle had taken her virginity the night before she was killed. He said she had virtually fled from him the morning after they had sex because she felt what they had done was wrong; she needed to repent. She had wanted to save herself for marriage, Kyle said. Knowing this, he still decided to coax her into his bed with promises of marriage and a future together.

I had kept calm for only long enough after he told me this so that I could get the final bit of information from him about where Lily went. The only place he could think was that she would have tried to find Father Donovan. As he has a room at the motel that he has permanently occupied since becoming the preacher here, she might have tried to come here.

This is crucial information, information that can help me find out where Lily went and why she was murdered. Why the hell did he keep it from me?! None of this information was in Lily's case file. This means Kyle didn't tell Ethan or any of the other investigating officers about this when he was interviewed.

I look around my motel room wildly, needing to punch or break something, but nothing immediately registers as a possible offering to my anger.

Focus, Mia, focus!

Drawing a deep breath, I fight my anger into submission.

Focus.

First, I need to find out if Lily came to the motel, as Kyle suspects, and get a list of guests who stayed at the motel on the day Lily was murdered to see if any of the guests stand out as possible murder suspects.

Second, I need to get into Mr. Reynolds' phone and track down that URL.

Third, I need to speak to more family members and friends of the victims to see if any of them saw any changed behavior, any strange trips that were taken, or if the victims had perhaps accessed the same paper as Mr. Reynolds.

Taking another deep breath, I focus on my plan and the steps I need to take next.

I turn on my heel to go and find Adam, but as I look out and see the stars shimmering outside the window, I realize the time.

I guess I will need to put my plan into action tomorrow morning first thing. But for now, I need to sleep, and I can only hope my dreams will not be full of the anger I am feeling.

# Chapter 8:

I still feel angry and agitated as I get up, later than my usual 7 AM, and groggy from the drinks last night.

Sleeping late has not helped my mood after last night, and now I am hungry as well as angry: a perfect storm to start my day.

I check my phone and see that Kyle tried to call me a few times, and there are voice and text messages from him asking me to call him and apologizing for keeping the information from me. His voice sounds worried and panicked.

I growl at my phone and the many messages and missed calls, and I grab my things to get ready in the bathroom.

Thirty minutes later, I feel somewhat better. Perhaps not less angry or hungry, but clean, fresh, and ready to take on my to-do list.

Adam isn't at the front desk of the motel, and I realize it is Saturday. He's probably at church this morning for the kids' group that gathers there for activities.

My grumbling stomach reminds me that I need to get food just as my phone rings in my back pocket. I briefly check the screen to make sure it isn't Kyle before I answer.

"Hi, Ethan."

"Mia, are you at the motel?"

I sigh internally. No matter how attractive he is or how silky his voice is, I would appreciate a proper greeting every now and then.

"Yes, I'm on my way to get breakfast. I was going to call you as soon as I was done."

"No need. I'm on my way to pick you up. We can talk over breakfast."

Click. Silence.

I guess I'm being picked up for breakfast.

Sitting across from Ethan in the diner, I sip my coffee slowly, waiting for him to respond.

I had told him about my conversation with Mrs. Reynolds and the unfortunate but helpful outcome of my conversation with Kyle. Ethan hadn't said a word during the time I spoke, but his anger at Kyle had been palpable. Ethan had not been the one who had interviewed Kyle after Lily's murder, and I can see the wheels in his mind turning as he considers the implications of the information that was never shared with them, with the police, and the implications of what could have been found earlier.

Our server brings over our plates of food just as my stomach rumbles again. The food smells amazing, and I dig in, still waiting for Ethan to process the information and respond.

As Ethan picks up his fork, looking down at his plate, he finally speaks.

"I would like to help you with an item on your list. If you can get the list from Adam and get onto Mr. Reynolds' phone, I am happy to speak to the other victims' families and friends to see if there is a pattern to the behavior of the victims leading up to their deaths. It might be quicker if we divide to try and conquer."

No comment about Kyle yet. Interesting... or perhaps he doesn't know how to comment.

"If you are happy to do the interviews with family and friends, I would appreciate it. I am not sure how long it will take me to find the information on Mr. Reynolds' phone, although I am hoping that he wasn't tech-savvy, and I can access the details easily. But first, I need to get that list from Adam."

I take another bite of my food, and Ethan does the same as he nods his agreement to my comment.

Eating in silence for a few moments, I go through my list and the information that is still outstanding.

"You know, we still need those medical files and histories from Kyle. I hope he gets it soon. The less I need to work with him, the better."

At my words, Ethan looks up to study my face, swallowing his food.

"Mia, I know you are angry with me, but you might need to consider that he probably didn't mean any harm, nor did he know that it is vital information. And it could have been awkward, telling the police that you were dumped just after having sex for the first time with a woman you had been dating for a few months."

My full stomach and the good coffee have helped to improve my mood. I mull Ethan's words over, trying not to dismiss the explanation outright.

I guess that it could be true. Kyle might have been embarrassed. After all, he's the town bad boy, the stud who has bedded half the women below 30 (and even some over) in this town and the surrounding towns. Having your girlfriend dump you the morning after the two of you have sex for the first time cannot be good for the ego.

I might feel a bit of happiness at this.

Ethan accompanies me back to the motel room to grab the details of the other victims' families, starting with the ones in town.

Walking into my room, I feel Ethan's attention go to my makeshift board against the closet doors.

Turning, I see him frowning at the messages in the middle, knowing that the two messages are of vital importance. If only we can figure out what they mean.

As he frowns at my board, I write down the details of the three families in town that he can visit to see if he can get any additional information from them.

"Here," I say as I hand the information to Ethan. "I am not sure how many of them will be willing to speak to you about the so-called accidents, but if we can confirm any similarities in their lives to the few weeks before Mr. Reynolds died, it will help us connect the dots more clearly and form a picture of why these people were murdered."

Taking the page from my hand, Ethan nods his agreement and turns toward me, but before he can say a word, his phone rings. Why are we forever being interrupted by phones?

"Detective Hayes. Morning. Yes, I am here at the moment. No, I need to get to work. Yes? I see. I can come get the files from you, thanks."

Ethan pauses for a while, listening to whoever is on the other end of the phone, as he looks at me, brooding once again.

"That might be a good idea, yes. Where do you want to meet? All right, we will see you then."

We? He better not have just made plans on my behalf without confirming or even checking with me.

"That was Kyle. He has all the medical files that we requested and wants to meet up to go through them. He says he found some details that could be helpful. He asked if we could meet here in your room to go through everything this afternoon. I said yes."

What is it with this man and deciding what I should do and when?

I glower at Ethan, not in the slightest feeling in the mood to entertain Kyle, especially not here in my room.

"I only have one chair and a bed. Where is he going to sit?" I reply flatly, trying to get out of this arrangement. I know we cannot meet in a public place to discuss medical files, but I do not want Kyle in my room... not after his revelations last night.

"I will find another chair for us to use. It shouldn't be too difficult; otherwise, I am happy to sit on the floor."

I realize Ethan isn't going to give in, and the work needs to be done.

"Fine. I'm going to see if Adam is back yet. I want to get that list."

Leaving Ethan in my room to his own devices, I walk to the front desk, hoping that Adam has returned from his duties at the church.

I catch Adam just as he sits down at the front desk, waking the computer from sleep mode.

"Hi, Adam. How are you today?"

I try to keep my voice as light and friendly as possible. Perhaps honey will trap more flies than vinegar today.

"Mia, hello. I'm okay. And you? Is everything okay?"

Adam looks as surprised to see me as he did when I first gave him my name two days ago upon arrival. Perhaps he is surprised that I would want to speak to him.

"I'm doing well, thanks. And yeah, no problems at all. I was just wondering about your booking system. Has it always been digital, or did you used to do book-ins by hand for visitors?"

His eyes narrow slightly at my line of questioning, and I see his face close off a bit, as though he does not want to show any emotion about my questions or where they might be leading.

"The church got the system set up about six years ago when we got a website. Before then, we used to write it all down. Is there something specific you're looking for?"

Perfect, this might just work to my advantage.

"I was hoping to try and find a guest, a friend of mine, who stayed here around five years ago, in June. You wouldn't be able to give me the details of the guests who stayed here, please?"

I smile sweetly at Adam as I lean towards him over the front desk, hoping that the older man isn't used to young women subtly flirting with him and that I can twist his arm with a few smiles and compliments.

Unfortunately, his only reaction is to narrow his eyes. This isn't working.

Luckily, there is always Plan B. My favorite plan. Hacking.

"I am sorry, but I cannot give you that information. It is against the law. I would think an FBI agent knows that."

"Of course, I completely understand," I say, still smiling. "Thank you so much in any way, Adam. Enjoy the rest of your day."

I throw a last smile his way before I turn back to my room.

Kyle had started apologizing the moment I had opened my room door for him, and I had held up a hand to stop the torrent of words. I am still angry, but I can understand why he might not have thought it was critical information to share.

Since I didn't murder him on sight, he sighed, relieved, and proceeded into my room, seating himself on the chair that Ethan had found somewhere.

Now, the three of us sit with the medical reports and histories Kyle had pulled.

"There is one file, in particular, that I want to show you that seemed strange to me. Natalie Keen. She should have had pain medication show up in her toxicology report, as she was on quite a strong dose at the time of her death. It was prescribed to her for a bad shoulder injury, and the medication was specifically without any opioids, as it seems she was a former drug addict."

Ethan's face turns whiter and whiter while Kyle speaks, and he looks down at his feet when he sees my eyes on him.

Firming my resolve and letting all my previous suspicions color my voice, I turn to Ethan to ask my question.

"Ethan, you knew Natalie. We spoke about it before. Do you know why the medication did not show up on her toxicology report? There was also no mention of an injured shoulder in the post-mortem report that I can remember. Do you know why?"

Ethan shuffles his feet, sighs, and wipes a hand across his face.

"I always knew this would come back to haunt me; I just didn't know how, and now, here it is."

Kyle flicks his gaze to me, puzzled, but I keep my attention focused on Ethan, giving him the time to gather his thoughts and speak.

"Natalie was a recovering drug addict, and I had bribed the medical examiner to leave the drugs that were found in her system off her report. Her family was already in mourning when she died. They didn't need to think she had relapsed as well. She was dead. I didn't think it would make a difference."

My shock at Ethan's admission of bribery is mirrored by Kyle as we look at each other and then back at Ethan.

"So, for the last two days, every time I said that Natalie Keen doesn't fit in with the other victims due to the toxicology... You just left it at that? Ethan, this means she ties in perfectly with the other victims; she fits the profile. Why would you keep this from me?"

His already brooding face becomes darker at my words, and he locks his eyes onto mine.

"I didn't try to keep this from you on purpose, Mia. I have been living with this lie for so long that I didn't know how to bring it up or explain why I did it without you not trusting me. You and Kyle, for that matter."

Ethan nods towards Kyle as he speaks of Kyle, but his eyes stay fixed on me.

Waiting, I know, for my reaction and words.

He had lied to me and omitted vital information that could have helped me make sense of a piece of the puzzle two days ago already.

Has it really been only two days? Time seems to be moving incredibly slowly and, in the same breath, way too fast while I am here in Cedarwood.

I need a break.

A break from these two, Ethan and Kyle.

I think it's time for me to investigate a bit deeper solo with my own special methods.

I force myself to focus on the two men in front of me, both waiting for me to reply.

# Chapter 9:

"Thank you for the reports and information, Kyle. I appreciate your help with it. For now, though, I think it best if you both leave. I need a break to digest all the information you gave me and what we have found so far. And I need a bit of time on my own."

I look them both in the eye as I use a slightly watered-down version of my FBI agent voice to make sure they know exactly how serious I am; no back talk will be allowed, nor are they welcome to stay in my room longer.

As I get up from the bed to open the door for the two of them to leave, Ethan is first to speak.

"Mia, I am sorry for keeping the truth from you. For not being honest about Natalie from the start. I was simply trying to keep a grieving family from being further devastated by having tainted memories of their daughter who had died. I have no other defense than this, and I can only hope that you understand why I did what I did to protect the memory of my friend."

Holding the door open, I keep my eyes on his face. The openness and honesty of his words are plain to see there.

But it is a little too late at the moment. I need to process, and I need to get this frustration out of my body and mind. Both these men omitted important information, both of them impeding my investigation. Good intentions or not, I am still pissed.

"Ethan, I understand, but I need you to leave. I want to be alone. I'll call you on Monday. The same for you, Kyle. I know you did not purposefully try to keep the information regarding Lily from me, but I need to have some time to myself. Please leave."

Ethan gives me a final, unhappy glance but leaves without a word.

"I really am sorry, Mia," Kyle says as he walks past me. "I hope you can forgive me."

I shut the door; my energy suddenly gone. I look around at the mess of files and papers scattered across my room.

There is no way in hell I am packing anything up now. I have some hacking to do.

Breaking into the booking system for the motel had been a breeze. A toddler could have done it, and the information regarding the guests booked in at the motel was now waiting for me to dissect it.

But first I need to get the information from Mr. Reynolds' phone. I had plugged the phone in to charge earlier, and I now turned it on, unlocking it with the code that was given.

Opening the browser, I check the browser history. Empty.

So, Mr. Reynolds had indeed known at least one thing about technology. Unfortunately for him, simply clearing his browser history won't stop me from finding what he was looking at.

I plug the phone into my laptop, and with a few keystrokes, I am in the backend of Mr. Reynolds' online profile. All its details are laid bare.

Ignoring the massive number of searches for porn and some strange searches for how to cover bruises, I filter the results until I find the URL I am looking for a paper published by Toronto University on the Day of the Dead. The document is 105 pages long and not as academic as one might expect.

Before I can make sure if this is indeed the key, I need to find out if any of the other victims had also visited this URL.

Grabbing the nearest file, I look for an email address that I can hack. There's nothing in the first file, but the second file has some details.

It takes me a few minutes longer to get into Anna Jordan's profile, but it isn't long before I can view all her secrets. She ran a lucrative pay-per-view porn profile in her spare time, it seems. Goodness, Anna, what else might you be hiding?

As I go through the details in her search history, I find the same URL.

Trying to contain my excitement, I grab another file. I need to confirm that this is indeed the key I am looking for with a third test.

I go through a few files before I find another email address, this time for Leeroy Smith. Hacking into his account, I realize this one might take a moment or two longer. Leeroy had more than one account, and on each of these, he had an online gambling account with a different website. He was in an enormous amount of debt. I wonder how his family can afford to pay it back. The financial strain must be massive.

A few more strokes and I find the same URL, confirming that I have the key... or at least what I think is the key.

The only way to be sure is to take the messages and decipher them using the online paper and see if it works.

I try various methods to crack the key and make sense of the messages, and I am fourth time lucky: the first number in each row references the page number. The numbers after that indicate the word to use to get the message.

With the paper open on half of my laptop screen and the messages on the other half, I follow the pattern to unlock the messages:

*Día de los Muertos*
*Repent, and your sins will be forgiven*
*43 9 15 91 3*
*Collection harbor Two days*
*90 14 112 35*
*Deliver 24 hours*
*20 50 72 18*
*Back road only*
*101 11 85 44*
*new details follow*
*61 1 164*
*two weeks*
*Día de los Muertos*

*Forgiveness is yours to receive*
*7 67 109*
*Two days*
*95 10 87*
*Motel noon*
*31 77 12 90 21*
*Come alone or else*

I sit back, staring at the messages.

Instructions to collect and deliver something and a message that led to their deaths. What had these people collected that caused them to end up dead?

Also, the "Come alone or else" at the end was a definite threat.

Someone had blackmailed these people into doing some or other delivery and then simply killed them when the job was done.

The reference to sins and repenting in both messages is also bugging me. The repetition has to mean something; it has to be pointing to something specific.

I cast eyes at my makeshift board and all the faces stuck there. Someone had meticulously selected all of these people, seemingly blackmailed them, and then discarded them when they were no longer useful.

Who, why, and how are the questions I need to answer now.

First, which harbor is the message referencing? For this, I will need GPS data.

Going back to Leeroy's profiles, I search through his inboxes for the details I need.

Yes, there! He had a GPS tracker installed in his car: perfect for me to find out where he had been two weeks and two days before he died.

I get to work on the GPS data, determined to find more details immediately, although I know it will take a few minutes, maybe even an hour, to hack the car tracking company's server.

To my surprise, the server is not nearly as secure as it should be for a company that hosts GPS data. I ponder this as I find the right account and pull the details to see where Leeroy had gone.

New York Harbor?

That was a ten-hour drive from here, not just around the corner.

I check Mr. Reynolds' phone GPS data for information on where he went.

Also New York Harbor.

No wonder Mrs. Reynolds saw that much of a jump on the odometer in their truck.

I need to check Anna's GPS data as well and I go back into her profile.

Yes, there: also New York Harbor.

I want to say this is the end, but I will need to check where each of the victims went to confirm, if it was New York Harbor, I know just the person to call for assistance. First, though, I need all the evidence I can get.

The sky is pitch black outside by the time I look up from my laptop screen. My eyes are sore, my back stiff, and my fingers cramping from typing with great haste.

But I have all the answers I wanted.

Every single one of the victims had made a trip to New York Harbor exactly two days and two weeks before they had died. They had driven there and back within a twenty-four-hour period, and all of them had stopped at the Joseph family farm just outside of town when they got back.

The only thing I know about the Josephs is that their son, Edgar, had dared me to hack a server for the FBI or DEA. If it wasn't for that asshole, I would never have been taken away.

Perhaps I should thank him for helping make sure I did not spend my entire life in this forsaken town.

Pulling my thoughts back to the information in front of me, I take stock of all the details.

If all the clues are pointing at the Joseph family farm, I will need to visit it.

I grab my keys, wallet, and phone as I get up, determined now that I have made up my mind what to do. I should probably not enjoy breaking and entering as much as I do, but the slight thrill of the chase and danger go through me as I get into my car and head out to the farm.

I will need to park far enough away so that my headlights aren't visible to anyone on the farm. This will be much better as a surprise visit that no one knows of, and I am sure at night I will be able to explore more uninterrupted than during the day.

I am in luck as there is a new picnic spot next to the road close to the entrance to the farm, and I park my car there, making sure to lock it behind me. I have the flashlight, my phone (on silent), a flick knife, and pepper spray in my pockets. I don't know what is waiting for me, but I would rather be ready than surprised.

Staying in the shadows of the trees, I make my way to the farmstead and barns. Luckily, they are not too far from the main road, although obscured by the line of massive old trees.

I keep my fingers crossed that there are no dogs on the farmyard as I approach, but all seems quiet. There are still lights on in the house, but they seem to be on only in one bedroom of the house.

Making my way towards the barns, I see a light on in the one furthest from me. Why would anyone be in a barn this time of the night? As far as I know, farmers do not leave lights on for their animals.

I walk closer slowly and carefully, keeping as quiet as possible. I cannot use my flashlight out of fear that it will be seen, and walking blind is not easy.

Voices carry out to me from the barn, and I peer through the gaps around the door frame. I cannot see anything clearly, though, and take a risk by moving closer to the open doors.

Sitting around a collapsible table are three men, one of whom is Edgar. They're drinking, talking, and counting money.

I try to move a bit closer to get a better look, and my foot hits a rock or something by the door. I cringe at the sound, as the talking inside dies down.

"You hear that?" one of the voices from inside says.

I need to get out of here, and fast. Swinging around, I hug the shadows of the barns and duck into the narrow alley between the two further barns just as a head pops out from the door I had been standing at moments before.

Daring a look, I peep around the corner and see the man step outside the barn, a gun in his hand.

"Must have been one of the cats again. Can't see anything. Fucking cats, man."

Laughter from inside the barn joins his laugh as he steps back inside.

I sigh in relief as he retreats into the barn.

I need to get back to my car and then make a plan to get into that barn during the day.

Perhaps a little reunion with Edgar needs to be arranged.

# **Chapter 10:**

I had told Ethan and Kyle that I would phone them on Monday to give myself a day to process all that had happened, but sitting here in the coffee shop, having breakfast and digesting the night before, I wonder if I should message Ethan and Kyle and inform them of what I found.

I savor the last bite of my chocolate chip pancakes, thoughts milling about in my head.

Kyle had been friends with Edgar Jones at school when I had left town, so perhaps he could help us get invited to the farm. I definitely should have taken Angie up on her offer to sign out a firearm, but for now, Ethan's assistance will need to be enough. At least I had listened when Angie had forced me to do additional field training when I started working full time for the Bureau, even though I only work in the office.

With a sigh, I take a sip of my coffee and pull out my phone to send two texts.

Ethan and Kyle both reply within minutes of receiving my message, and I sit in the coffee shop, waiting for them to show up. Perhaps having extra coffee while talking to them will help me deal with them more calmly.

As I sit staring out the window at the slow, small-town traffic outside, both Ethan and Kyle pull up simultaneously, exchanging a nod in greeting as they exit their cars, no words. Men.

Entering the coffee shop, Kyle's eyes dart around, but Ethan's eyes immediately focus on me: brooding, dark, mesmerizing as he walks to my table.

"Hi, Mia. I'm so glad you texted."

The spell that had kept my eyes fixed on Ethan's breaks as Kyle greets me, and I look up at him.

"Hi, Kyle, Ethan. Thanks for coming on short notice, but I found a few things last night that we need to discuss. Sit, please."

I call the server over as they take a seat, and Ethan only nods at me in acknowledgment—no verbal greeting.

With a coffee in front of each of us, I take a deep breath and look up at their expectant faces. Kyle's face is open and anticipatory; Ethan is brooding again, serious.

"Yesterday after you left, I... I had to... I couldn't let the thought of the paper on Mexico and the additional miles on Mr. Reynold's truck go, so I decided to dig into details further and found quite a lot. I could confirm that all the victims had visited that same paper published about Mexico, and I was able to dig into the GPS data for over half of the victims. All of them had driven to the New York harbor and back exactly two weeks and two days before they were killed."

I pause, watching the information sink in for both Ethan and Kyle. Kyle's face is an open book, and I can read every emotion running across it as I speak, but Ethan is more of a statue. His usual brooding look seems to have frozen on his face, and the only sign of any emotion is his frown which deepens as I speak.

Both seem to be on the verge of asking questions, and I hold up a hand to stop them.

"I also found that on their way back, each of the victims I could track had stopped at the Jones's farm. I suspect to deliver whatever it is they had collected at the harbor or to receive payment. After I made this connection, I drove out to the Jones's farm last night to see if I could find anything obvious there, and I saw Edgar and two other men sitting in one of the barns counting money. I accidentally knocked something with my foot and had to hide, but Edgar came out holding a gun, which tells me the money was not donations they received from kind strangers."

Ethan and Kyle start to protest against my actions and the danger I have been in, but I silence them.

"After your omissions, I was not going to call either of you; I needed the alone time. I actually still feel like I need some time to myself, but the investigation is more important than my feelings regarding your actions. Plus, no one saw me or knew that I was there. And I would like to remind you both that I am an FBI agent and am more than capable of looking after myself. So, keep your protests to yourself, please."

I see the words die in their mouths and their egos deflate somewhat at my words. Kyle's face is turning slightly red at the admonishment, and Ethan is furrowing his brow so much that I am pretty sure a pencil might be able to stay lodged in the wrinkles. The ridiculous thought of playing with Ethan's furrowed brow crossing my mind almost has me giggling, but I shake the thought off and clamp down on my reaction.

"Look, the reason I messaged you is, Kyle, you were friends with Edgar in school. Is there any information you have about the Joneses and Edgar that can help all this make sense?"

Ethan stares at me intently as I finish speaking, and I hold his intense gaze for a few moments before Kyle clears his throat.

"Edgar and I drifted apart towards the end of high school, but I know his family has always farmed with the same grains and cattle. Even now, they are still farming the same grains and cattle on their lands. Edgar was a bit of a troublemaker in high school and ended up in the principal's office as well as a police car more than a few times. Nothing ever stuck, though, as far as I know."

I look to Ethan at this to see if he has any comments about the run-ins with the police.

"There is nothing that I know of that Edgar Jones has been charged with, and he hasn't made trouble in quite a few years. I heard that he does have friends who are suspected to be part of the Sampson Smugglers, a gang that works with the cartels and smuggles anything from drugs to people to stolen art, but there is nothing else that I know of at present."

A lightbulb goes off in my head at the name "Sampson Smugglers." We had been tracking their activity about two years ago, but I was unable to make much progress as they do almost everything in old-school ways. No smartphones, no traceable vehicles, no paperwork left behind, and the books for Sampson & Co are squeaky clean. Annoyingly so.

Perhaps Lily's murder can help me solve more than just one mystery.

Focus, Mia.

One thing, one case, at a time.

I look at Ethan.

"Are you up for a night shift?

Kyle is not happy to be left out, but Ethan and I both agree that his coming with us to pay a visit to the farm would not be a good idea. Kyle might be fit and well-built, but he has no experience with weapons or defending himself in hand-to-hand combat.

I agree to meet Ethan outside the motel just after dark and wave him and Kyle off as we exit the coffee shop.

Getting into my car, the day stretches ahead of me. It is still a long time until dark, and I was so focused last night that my brain is feeling a bit smushed today.

I need some physical exercise, to kick or punch something.

I grab my phone and look up the operating hours for the local gym, keeping my fingers crossed for some good news.

Open on Sundays.

Perfect.

Waiting outside the motel for Ethan in my black jeans, sneakers, and a black t-shirt, I silently thank the gym owner for having a spare set of gloves for me to use earlier today. The forty-five minutes of bag work was exactly what I needed to calm my soul.

Ethan pulls up, and I jump into the front seat.

"Ready?" Ethan asks as I fasten my seatbelt.

"Yes, let's go. I want to find out what is going on in that barn and on that farm."

The drive to the farm is quiet, but not unpleasantly so. Ethan has classic rock music playing from his phone in the car, and I listen in surprise. I am not sure what type of music I thought he might listen to, but it wasn't this.

I show Ethan where I had parked last night, and he pulls off the road in the same spot.

"I should go first; you bring up the rear," he says as he turns to me.

Scowling at Ethan, I retort, "I'm the one who was here last night and knows where to go. When last were you on this farm?"

Ethan scowls back at me, but I can see my logic defeating his urge to be in the lead.

Without waiting for an answer, I get out of the car and walk around to the tree line so that I can follow the same path I did last night.

Ethan stops me with a gentle hand on my arm, and I look up at him, pleasantly shocked by the touch.

"Here, take this; it's my personal weapon. I don't want you walking in without any protection."

I look down at his outstretched hand and the gun he is offering, holster, belt, and all.

Taking it, I feel a warmth spreading across my cheeks as I strap the belt across my hips and fit the holster to sit comfortably.

"Thank you, Ethan," I say softly. Clearing my throat, I continue, "Let's get going."

Getting to the barn tonight is easier as I know the path. As we get to the farmyard, I slow down, listening and watching for any movements. The house nor barns have lights on, and the yard is eerily quiet.

Keeping to the shadows again, I lead Ethan to the furthest barn, where I saw the men counting money last night.

There is a padded lock on the door, and Ethan sighs, looking at it.

"Don't worry. I got this," I whisper to him as I drop to my knees, remove two pins from my pocket, and start picking the lock.

I can feel the curiosity radiating from Ethan at my lock-picking skills, but the lock pops open, and his attention shifts to the interior of the barn as I slide open one of the doors just enough for us to get inside.

The interior is so dark that I cannot see my hand. I take out my phone to put on the flashlight, and Ethan does the same.

"Let's split up and see what we can find. There are no windows in the barn, so we should be safe with the lights on for a while at least."

Ethan nods at me and turns to the left side of the barn as I move to the right.

After a few minutes of searching, Ethan flashes his light towards me.

"Here," he says, gesturing to the floor as I approach. "It's a locked trap door. Can you pick it?"

I grin at him, dropping to my knees again and picking the lock.

Carefully, I lift the trap door as Ethan keeps his light steady, revealing a basement-like space under one side of the barn with steps leading down.

Ethan climbs down the steps first, and I follow.

As I reach the bottom step, Ethan turns around, seemingly expecting me to still be in the barn above, and I step right into him. His arms fold around me, steadying me as I am knocked off balance.

His arms around me are strong, and the smell of him this close to me... I feel a bit dizzy as I look up at Ethan, just making out his expression in the dim light of our phones. His eyes are somewhat hazy in addition to their usual broodiness as he stares down at me.

I lick my dry lips and see Ethan's gaze follow the motion of my tongue. I open my mouth to say something, although I do not know what.

"Are you okay?" Ethan asks as he flicks his eyes away and steps back. I nod my confirmation, unable to reply, and I lower my gaze.

As Ethan turns away from me, I shake off the last cobwebs of the moment and look around.

Dozens of wooden crates are standing around in the basement area, most nailed shut, but there are a few that do not have lids.

We both turn to the open crates, lifting our phones to see inside.

Ethan and I look at each other in confusion.

Bibles. There are bibles in the crates.

I reach out to lift the bibles, but the crunch of tires on gravel warns us that someone is approaching.

We turn to the stairs, racing up them and popping the lock back in place on the trap door.

Back in the car, I breathe out in relief and lean my head against the seat as Ethan also sighs next to me.

"That was close, and the crates are interesting," Ethan murmurs, and I turn my head to him, pondering his strange statement.

"That was close, yes, but at least now we know something strange is going on and where it is happening."

"Hmm," is the only reply I receive as Ethan turns his head to look at me as well, his eyes trailing over me, meeting my gaze.

As we look at each other, I feel tension building up in my chest, and Ethan's breathing picks up ever so slightly.

A truck honking in the distance breaks the spell, bringing me back to reality, to where we are at present.

The silence in the car on the way back to the motel is heavier than before, as though we both are waiting for the other to say something. To admit the tension, the heat.

Or am I imagining all of this?

# Chapter 11:

I don't sleep all that well, and my mood is even less improved when I check my phone and realize I never plugged it in to charge.

Great, just what I need to start my day with.

Grabbing my charger, I plug in my phone and wait for the little battery icon to pop up so that I can switch it on.

As my phone goes through its processes to switch on, I let my mind wander to the previous evening, and what Ethan and I found in the basement of the barn.

Why bibles? And who oversees the operation? Whatever it may be.

As far as I can remember, Edgar Jones is not exactly the sharpest tool in the shed, so logic tells me he cannot be the one leading the operation.

My phone finally dings to life, and I wait as a few messages and notifications pop up.

A few notifications for emails, Instagram, and automated searches I have running for cases. Angie checking in to see how I am. Kyle messaging to hear if we found anything last night. And Ethan seeing if I am awake yet.

Hmm... I guess I need to reply to Ethan first, then the rest. Definitely need to reply to Angie as well.

I send Ethan a reply and grab my things to get ready for the day.

As I pull on my shoes, my phone beeps again. It's Ethan, inviting me to breakfast at the Raven Diner. He wants to talk.

Well, I *am* hungry.

Savoring my breakfast and warm coffee, I wait for Ethan to bring up what he has on his mind. He seems to be brooding even more than usual, and I leave him to decide in his own time when he wants to talk.

"Mia, I think the clues you received might have been to make sure we do not look at other incidents as well."

I look up at Ethan in surprise at the statement. That was certainly not what I was expecting him to say.

"What do you mean? Have there been other incidents and accidents that you think could be related to Lily's murder and the other victims?"

Ethan looks down at his coffee, frowning, as though he is deciding how much he should tell me.

"Ethan, I need you to tell me everything if you suspect there is more to this case. You agreed that we wouldn't have any secrets from the beginning, and you already concealed the truth about Natalie Keen. Please do not do something like that again, not now."

A confirmational harrumph is all I receive in reply as he continues to stare down his coffee.

Looking at him, I see the brooding eyes and the frown lines, but also the beautiful mouth and the long lashes. *It's so unfair that he has such gorgeous lashes*, I think to myself, just as he looks up to speak again.

"There are a few incidents that have occurred over the last few years that have gone unsolved or did not make sense to me, but I feel that they might tie in with Lily's murder and with last night. With all of it. Somehow."

Looking over his shoulder at the rest of the diner to see if anyone is close or listening, Ethan leans in towards me.

"There was a burned-out panel van with two unidentified bodies just over a year and a half ago. They seemed to be transporting crates of some sort. But the crates were completely burned, including the contents, and we were unable to identify what they were transporting, only what size they might have been due to the metal brackets that were left behind. The fire marshal concluded that an accelerant of some sort might have been used to burn the victims and the crates, and we have still not been able to identify the two victims. Meaning, it has led nowhere."

I frown at Ethan. How is it possible that there are so many incidents in and around all these small towns?

"We also had a fire at the motel, and the fire alarm failed, about a month after Lily's murder. And now that we know that is where she might have possibly gone there in search of Father Donovan, it stands to reason that someone might have been trying to destroy evidence. To make sure we wouldn't find out that she had been there."

A chill runs down my spine at Ethan's words. I need to go through the guest list I got from the motel's booking system again and the file on the burned panel van.

"Ethan, I need to get back to the motel. I need to go over the guest list again. Right now. But I also need the files on the panel van and the motel. Will you bring them to the motel to go over?"

I start getting up, but Ethan stops me.

"Mia, something sinister is going on here, and there are way too many similarities and coincidences for any of this to be accidental. You need to be careful; we need to be careful."

I stare at Ethan, my mind racing as I process the information and try and fit it in with all the other information we have uncovered.

"I'll get the check. Meet me back at the motel with the files as soon as you can."

Something dark is happening in this town and to its people, and I need to put a stop to it.

Ethan gave me the files to go over, and the details of the motel fire are so similar to the so-called accidents that I immediately know they are connected: meaning that everything is also connected to Lily.

Before Ethan arrived, I had repeatedly reviewed the guest list. But as only five other people, in addition to Father Donovan were staying in the motel on the day Lily disappeared, this had led me nowhere. Three were German tourists who had arrived late the afternoon on the day Lily disappeared, and the other two people were a mother and young son.

The only other people who had been here or could have been here from the evidence before me were Adam and Father Donovan, and that was only if Father Donovan was in his room and not about town or at the church. I wonder...

Perhaps I should probe Ethan and hear what his thoughts are on them.

"Adam," I ask Ethan, "what do you think of him?"

Lifting his eyebrows in surprise, Ethan flicks his eyes toward me.

"He is a bit strange and somewhat of a loner but incredibly devout and does whatever he can for the church and the church community. Has been since I arrived in town. He can be a bit closed off at times, and his only friend seems to be Father Donovan."

Yes, that seems to be the Adam I remembered, except that he had not been friends with the previous preacher. For him to be friends with Father Donovan, something must be different.

"I see... And Father Donovan?"

The preacher had been called to the church shortly after I had left Cedarwood, and I did not learn much about him. Nor was I much of the church-going type towards the end of my time here, so I highly doubt I would have known him well now even if I had stayed in town.

"Father Donovan is involved in the community and often does home visits to keep in touch with the people who attend church, even the casual churchgoers and the farmers. People seem to like him in general, and I haven't heard of anyone complaining about him or his sermons. Except perhaps a few of the older generation who aren't too impressed about the rumor that he has tattoos."

I sigh. This feels like a dead end, or my mind is somewhat overwhelmed. I am not sure. I need to go through the facts again and add more details to my makeshift board.

We don't have much time before the next accident might be taking place, and we have nothing solid yet.

I need to find concrete proof; I need to make headway.

Knowing of these two additional incidents on top of the other accidents is chilling. Who could be doing all of this? And why?

Focus, Mia.

The answers are here somewhere.

Focus.

# Chapter 12:

Ethan and I had gone over the files again and again, trying to find any additional information.

I added more photos from the files to my makeshift board and notes to help me keep track of the information and connections between incidents.

There must be a connection somewhere in all of this, one person who can tie it all together.

"I need to go to the station."

Ethan's voice startles me from my staring contest with the board, and I turn to look at him.

"Oh, yeah, sure. I will keep going on here, and you can let me know if there is anything else you find or can think of regarding the incidents or victims."

Nodding his agreement, Ethan picks up his phone and keys and opens the door.

"I will let you... What the fuck?" Ethan exclaims as he takes a step back into the room.

"What?" I bristle. Why do men seemingly enjoy making me jump?

Ethan turns to me, his face dark with anger and something else that I cannot pinpoint.

"You can't stay here. Pack your things. You can stay at my place."

Frowning, I step closer to the door to see what Ethan is reacting to, and there, on my doorstep, is a Bible with a dead raven on top of it. A knife stuck through both; a scribbled note tied to the handle of the knife.

*Leave Cedarwood and call off the Detective.*

*Or we will come for you.*

"A tad dramatic, don't you think?" I sarcastically quip with the note in my hand as I turn to Ethan, his face becoming more thunderous at my words and tone. I lift my hands in an apology. "Sorry, sorry. I don't enjoy feeling like I am being forced into a corner. This is serious, of course, but I cannot leave the motel and stay with you over a few threats. This just means we are making progress and getting closer to the truth. And I would like to, once again, remind you that I am an FBI agent. A field-trained FBI agent."

"Either you pack your things, or I pack them. There are no security cameras in the motel, and anyone can walk in day or night. You are not staying here, Mia. Not a damn minute longer," his voice is dark with an edge to it. "We can work on the case from my place. There is more than enough space and a proper bedroom for you. You pack, or I pack. Choose."

Glaring at Ethan, I try to contain my irritation at his attitude and ultimatum while weighing the pros and cons of staying at the motel. I agree that the motel is not safe, but staying with Ethan...

"Is there not another bed and breakfast or an Airbnb in town that will have space?" I try. There has to be another option.

"No. No Airbnb, no bed and breakfast. And before you ask, the motel isn't safe either. You can either stay with me, or I can make you comfortable in one of the cells at the station. You choose."

I continue glaring at Ethan, trying to think of another option, a logical and safe option. Perhaps a cell at the station could work...

Sighing on the inside, I turn my face to the makeshift board and the files spread across the floor.

"Fine. You bag the bird and the bible; I'll pack my bag. And then we can pack up the files and my board. I am just warning you: I am not easy to live with and I will not be staying in some or other dump of a bachelor pad. If I see a dirty bathroom or kitchen, I am looking for another place to stay."

A lopsided grin is the only response I get from Ethan as he turns back to the message that was left on my doorstep to bag it.

Wow. This man is full of surprises, and pleasantly so.

Ethan's house is not what I expected. The two-bedroom house is well-maintained and the décor minimal but effective in the space. The bedroom Ethan shows me is decorated in shades of green and gray, complete with a Monstera Deliciosa growing in one corner.

Leading me back to the dining room, Ethan puts the box of files down on the table and looks at me.

"Make yourself comfortable. You can work here or in the living room, but Otis occupies the couches most of the day, so I would recommend the dining room table. Help yourself to anything in the kitchen."

The quizzical look on my face has him stopping for a moment.

"What? Is something wrong?"

"Who, or what, is Otis? And do I need to be worried about them?"

Looking slightly embarrassed, Ethan scratches his head, grinning.

"Otis is my cat. I adopted him with the name, and well, it stuck. And it fits him quite well. He is in and out of the house, though, so he won't be a bother. Except maybe tonight. He likes to cuddle."

I smile back at Ethan and his little boy grin, imagining him and Otis cuddling. This man is full of surprises. And pleasant surprises at that.

I pull out the files and recreate my board against the dining room wall. Stepping back, I look at the faces of all the victims who had died in the so-called accidents.

There has to be more that ties them to each other. More than the messages and accidents. Something that explains how they ended up receiving those messages in the first place.

I retrieve my laptop from the bedroom and settle in at the dining room table across from my board.

I need to dig deeper and find out more about these people and their lives. Privacy be damned; I need to find answers.

My head snaps up as the front door opens and closes, and I look up in surprise.

"Everything okay?" Ethan asks as he flicks the light on, frowning at me sitting in the dim light.

I blink at him in confusion, my eyes adjusting to the light and looking away from my laptop screen.

"Hi. Hello. Uhm, yes. All good, but I think I found something. And it is not good. I think I know how all the victims got pulled into making those deliveries."

Hanging his jacket over one of the dining room chairs, Ethan walks closer to look at my laptop over my shoulder.

"What did you find?"

Organizing my thoughts and pulling up the details I found and made a list of, I turn to look up at Ethan.

"Each one of the victims had secrets that they did not want to be found. Every single one of them. And someone knew of this and used it against them. Used it to blackmail them into doing those deliveries. I think that is what the 'or else' at the end of the second message each person received meant. They had to comply, or else their secrets would be made public."

Turning back to my laptop, I point to the list.

"Look, here. Mr. Reynolds, Kyle's dad, regularly beat Mrs. Reynolds and made sure that she hid it. Leeroy Smith had a massive gambling addiction and was hiding it from his family. Natalie Keen was being blackmailed with information about her advertising on a sugar daddy site years ago. I assume this was when she was still an active drug user, as the information is quite old. See? For every single one of these people, there is something similar that they have been hiding. Here, a child with another woman, another affair here. A hit-and-run that had been covered up. They were all being blackmailed. All of them!"

In my excitement at my findings, I realize too late that the details about Natalie might be upsetting to Ethan. I try to sneak a peek at his expression, but he has carefully crafted it into a mask. The only sign of emotion is a slight frown as he looks at the list I made.

"I wonder if Kyle knows about his father."

The quiet gentleness with which Ethan asks the question has me pausing for a moment.

"No," I replied contemplatively. "No, I don't think he knows. And I am sure his mom won't talk about it in front of him either. Kyle worships his dad, and I think his mom would want to make sure that the image Kyle has of his dad doesn't get tarnished."

"Should we talk to the families about what you found? It could upset quite a lot of people in town, but we need confirmation and answers to make sure this information is correct. That these people were not being blackmailed with fabricated evidence."

Frowning at my laptop screen, I nod in agreement.

"These are not going to be easy conversations to have with the families. A lot of people are going to be incredibly hurt and shocked."

I move to get up from the chair I had been sitting in for the last few hours, Ethan moving away to give me some space.

"You look like you need some food and a drink. Let's talk in the kitchen."

Otis finally makes his appearance during dinner and decides to stay right next to me on the couch, obviously hoping for something to eat.

Enjoying the last of my wine, I sit on the couch, stroking Otis and going over the details we had discussed during dinner. Splitting up the list of families to speak to had been easy enough, but deciding whether to involve Kyle in this was not. If he did not know about his dad assaulting his mom, we could risk derailing our investigation and losing his assistance and access to any additional medical details we might need.

Playing with Otis's fur, I let my mind wander, thinking of all the secrets that the victims kept, how many lives might be upended with the information, and how many more secrets there might still be in this town and the neighboring towns.

"You know, I think I should take Kyle with me for the visits to the families. I am mainly going to be speaking to people in town, and many of them only have memories of me as a juvenile delinquent being dragged away by the FBI. Perhaps his influence can soften some of the blows that need to be dealt. And... And if he doesn't know about his dad... Well, if he freaks out and abandons the investigation, then so be it, but this is too big to hide from him. He is part of the investigation. His family is part of the investigation. He should know."

Taking a deep sip from his beer, Ethan looks at Otis next to me, watching the cat enjoy scratches and purring loudly.

"You're right. But I think you should speak to him alone first, calm him down if he doesn't know about this and is upset, and then go talk to his mom. We don't want him bursting out in front of Mrs. Reynolds. It will be bad enough for her to have to relive the memories without her son making it worse."

I nod, still looking at Otis, enjoying the purrs and his warmth next to me. I've never been a cat person, but this roly-poly cat might just change my mind.

"I'll phone Kyle in the morning to meet up with him and go over what I found and what we discussed. I just hope he and all the other families can process the information about their loved ones without it damaging their memories of their loved ones."

As I sit in Mrs. Reynolds' living room again, the pain on Kyle's face and his mom's tears has me wishing I could be anywhere but here right now.

Kyle had listened to what I had to say calmly, much more calmly than I thought he would, and had agreed to help me meet with all the families. The only conditions were that we meet with his mom last and that we work around his schedule.

All the families have been spoken to, questions asked and answered. There had been many tears over the last two days, people screaming in hopelessness and pain, others quietly confirming that the blackmail details were the truth, horrified at having to relive the details.

And here we were now: Kyle hoping his mom would confirm the blackmail details as lies, only for her to confirm the opposite.

Mr. Reynolds had indeed been beating her for years, and she had been hiding it, staying with him in the hopes that he would change, staying for the sake of her children.

"Kyle, honey, I never wanted you or your sister to find out. Your father was a good man. He just... He would just get into a bit of a rage at times. And as long as he left you and Annette alone, I could live with it. Please, sweetheart, don't be angry with me for not saying anything."

The devastation on Kyle's face at his mom's words breaks my heart, and I look away as he stands up to hug her.

I have my answers, but I am not sure how many people in this town will be able to trust each other or their family members after all that has been revealed.

And I am not sure how many people I can trust either.

# Chapter 13:

I left Kyle at his mom's house so that they could talk and drive back to Ethan's place, the information I had gathered over the last two days in my laptop bag.

Ethan has been out to the neighboring towns, talking to families as well, and we have not seen much of each other over the last two days except for a quick chat over dinner last night to catch up with each other.

I am still trying to trace who had sent the emails with the blackmail details, but not having the time to sit and concentrate for longer than 30 minutes at a time, this has proven difficult. Tonight, though, I need to dig in and spend some proper time getting into that.

My phone dings as I pull into Ethan's driveway, and I briefly glance at the screen to see what it is. Barely registering the notification content as I get out of the car, my mind finally registers what it is. A new message has been posted on MasterOfAll's notification board.

Someone is being blackmailed right now and will be making a trip to New York Harbor in two days. Two days. I have two days to find out who this person is and who or what they are transporting.

Realizing that I am still standing in Ethan's driveway with one foot in my car, staring at my phone, I extricate myself from my car. My laptop. I need to get to my laptop.

As I hurry inside, Otis comes running from the side of the house to follow me in, greeting me loudly.

My laptop is still on the dining room table where I left it, and I immediately start searching for IP addresses accessing the message board. Someone has to log on and open up the message to read it.

My fingers flew across the keyboard, I put a tracker in place, waiting for someone to access the message.

While the code is running, I try to track MasterOfAll again. Whoever this is, they will slip up at some point, and I need to be there to catch them.

There. The IP address. MasterOfAll slipped up this time, or someone was doing their dirty work for them and did not conceal their tracks as well as MasterOfAll usually does.

I immediately run geolocation for the IP address to pinpoint it, and a location pops up.

What the...

No, this can't be right.

I run the geolocation again, keeping my eyes locked on my laptop screen.

Yes, the first trace was right.

The message was posted from within the motel. Someone at the motel is MasterOfAll or an accomplice.

I need to get there now. Right now.

As I grab my keys and my phone, the tracker I had put in place to find who accesses the message on the board flashes an IP address onto my screen.

Damn it, damn it, damn it.

Do I go to the motel and try and find MasterOfAll or do I track the next victim and get them to cooperate?

The choice is made for me when Ethan, followed by Kyle, steps into the house, not talking. Ethan looks grave, and Kyle... Kyle seems haunted. After what he learned today, no one can blame him.

Looking at me standing frozen in front of my laptop, keys, and phone in hand, Ethan asks, "Is everything okay?"

"I found the next victim, and I tracked where the newest message was posted from. It came from the motel."

Kyle's head whips up at this.

"You found the next victim? Who is it?"

His voice has a desperate edge to it, and his eyes seem almost wild for a moment.

"I was on my way to see if I can find MasterOfAll when…"

Kyle cuts me off, shaking his head. He walks to my laptop, looking at the screen past me, trying to see the information he is looking for on the screen.

"No. We need to find the victim first. They need help. Do you have an address?"

He tries to move me away from my laptop, but I stand firm.

"Kyle, stop. You are not touching my laptop, and we are going to discuss this calmly. Stand back and take a breath."

My suddenly firm voice seems to cut through whatever thoughts are racing through his mind, and Kyle steps back, an embarrassed look on his face.

"Mia, I think you need to explain what happened. Then we can decide which person to track. The person who posted as MasterOfAll might have simply been using the internet at the motel and left, but whoever accessed the message will be home judging by the time. Let's get all the information together and then decide on a course of action."

Ethan's calm words and logic have me fuming a little internally. I want to go after MasterOfAll right now, but his logic makes sense. I put my phone and keys down on the dining room table with a grumbled agreement.

Sitting down, I started explaining what I had found and how I had found it without going into too much technical detail.

As I read the address for the message recipient, Kyle and Ethan share a look.

"Do you know whose address this is? And if so, would you mind sharing the information?"

That shared look again.

Clearing his throat, Kyle says, "That is Ray Hickey's address. I don't know if you remember him from school, but he now works as a farm hand."

Ray Hickey is one of my sister's best friends. The guy she took with her everywhere but never dated. He wasn't hot enough according to her, but tolerable as a friend because his parents were rich, and he could always get concert tickets and new music and clothes for her when she wanted them.

"I see. Ray." I pause, trying to fight off the demons from the past and silencing my sister's voice in my head. "I guess we will need to pay him a visit. And sooner rather than later. Tonight."

Ethan stands up, taking his car keys out of his pocket, Kyle looks at me with sympathy, as though he knows what is going on in my mind. Strange, as I never thought of him as someone who might have realized what had happened to me at home. Or someone who would care, to be honest.

"I agree that we need to talk to Ray sooner rather than later. Let's go."

Ray's house looks exactly like the others around it: one of the small square houses in the newer part of town that are built in the style of a big-city townhouse. The quaint garden is neat, the hedges trimmed.

I observe all of this as we walk to the front door, Kyle ringing the bell. He seems to have calmed down, and the haunted look has mostly faded from his face.

Ray opens the door with a worried look on his face.

"Hi, Ray. How are you doing? Sorry for dropping by so late, but I was hoping you would let us in for a quick chat?" Kyle says in one breath as Ray stares at the three of us in front of his door.

"Kyle, hey. Uhm, sure, I guess. Come on in."

He steps away and opens the door wider for us to come in.

The inside of the house is neat as well, but impersonal. I cannot help but compare it to Ethan's house. Ethan's house was a home. This... this is simply a house. Nothing more.

Ray gestures for us to take a seat in the living room, nervously looking around.

Well, at least I know what he is nervous about. I can only hope he is willing to work with us so that we can catch whoever MasterOfAll is. And stop them.

"Ray, we are here for more than a casual chat. We need your assistance with an investigation."

Ethan's voice breaks through my musings, pulling me back to the present, and I see him looking at me pointedly. Waiting for me to explain further.

"I am sure by now you have heard from many people that I am in town on an investigation, and the investigation has led me, led us, to believe that your life is in danger. There is no easy way to ask this, so I am going to dive right in. Ray, did you receive a message to decipher from an online notification board posted by MasterOfAll late this afternoon?"

Ray blanches at my words, at the question, and starts nervously folding and unfolding his hands. He knows what I am talking about, but I need to put him at ease.

"You are not in any kind of trouble here. We are here to ask for your help. We need you to tell us if you know who MasterOfAll is or have any idea who they might be. And we need you to give us any additional information that you perhaps have about this person and who they may or may not be working with. Ray, it is extremely important. Your life and the lives of many others are at stake here. And if you can help us with this, we might be able to solve my sister Lily's murder."

The shock on Ray's face at the mention of Lily tells me that he did not know that is why I was in town or that it could be connected to his situation. Good, then the town has only been speculating about why I am here. The fewer people who know the truth, the better.

"Please, Ray, we are here to help, not judge," I press. "Whatever they have over you, we can help you with that. We just want to find MasterOfAll and make sure that no harm comes to you. Help us, please, and we will help you."

Sitting with my elbows on my knees, forward, keeping my eyes on Ray, I see various emotions run across his face. The most dominant one, though, and the one that stays, is fear.

"I... Uh, Mia, I..."

Clearing his throat, he tries again.

"Mia, thank you for the visit, but I do not know what you are talking about, and I would appreciate it if you left my house now. It is getting late, and I need to be up early to milk the cows. Mr. Adams does not appreciate things running late."

He gets up, clearly waiting for the three of us to do the same. Looking at Ethan and Kyle, who had been quiet through the exchange, I lift my eyebrows at them in a question and get up. Ethan and Kyle get up as well, and we move to the front door.

As we file out, Kyle turns back to Ray, sympathy and another emotion on his face.

"You know, Ray, you do not have to feel guilty about whatever they have on you. Mia and Ethan can genuinely help you. All you need to do is help them in return and be honest. If you want to make use of the assistance, phone me or Ethan. You are not alone."

Kyle's words seem to rattle Ray further, and he shuts the door in Kyle's face without bothering to say goodbye.

Back at Ethan's house, we all sit in the living room in silence, brooding.

"I think we need to follow him."

My voice breaks the silence, and the two men look up at me, Kyle surprised and Ethan calculating.

"I mean if he won't help us, and he doesn't want our help, then we use him to get the information we need. Following him won't be difficult, and we know that he will stop at the Jones's farm on the way back if he is doing the same trip that all the others did. I can follow him to New York Harbor and see who he meets there. Maybe find out what he is given to transport. Then one of you can wait at the Jones's farm, concealed, to see who he meets there to unload the transported goods."

Ethan and Kyle start protesting at the same time, and I hold a hand up to silence them.

"First off, you both have jobs, and you cannot simply up and leave. Second, I know New York and the harbor well. New York is my home. And third, I can handle myself. Ray will never know I am tailing him, and if I can identify who he meets with, we will be one step closer to finding out what the hell is going on in Cedarwood and the surrounding towns. If either of you can give me a solid, logical argument that contradicts anything I just said and that does not include the words 'but it is dangerous for you,' I am willing to listen. Otherwise, this is the plan, and we will be sticking to it. You can decide if only one of you or both of you want to keep watch at the Jones's farm. That I will leave up to you."

The sullen looks thrown in my direction tell me that neither of them has an argument for my logic or the plan as laid out. Good.

Downing the last bit of my beer, I get up, disturbing Otis from his snooze.

"Right, if you will excuse me, I need to go set up a tracker on the sat nav in Ray's truck and then go to bed. The tracker will alert me as soon as he is further than 10 miles from Cedarwood so that I know to follow."

"Mia, I do not like your plan, but I agree with it. Just... Be careful. You might be an FBI agent, but Ray is not just a victim at present; he is an adversary in his fearful state of mind."

I nod at Ethan, at his words, and walk to my laptop.

Focus, Mia.

Focus.

# Chapter 14:

It is a slow morning for me. No interviews to be had, no visits to make. Just waiting for the tracker on Ray's sat nav to alert me when he is on his way to New York.

Otis keeps me company as I hack into Ray's email to find what he is being blackmailed with. It is not much of a challenge to get in, and within minutes, the blackmail file is open in front of me.

No wonder he did not want our help. The file details Ray assaulting a woman one night at a dance in town. He had paid her off to keep her quiet, and she had left town within days of the incident.

Bastard.

Disgust causes a pit in my stomach as I read the details and see the photos included. How the hell was a case never opened when are there photos of the woman's bruises?

Maybe I don't want to stop an accident from happening to Ray.

No, I shake the thought from me. I need to keep my focus on the goal here. Ray will get what is coming to him once I hand the file over to Ethan and we have caught MasterOfAll.

I need a break, and I grab Otis to take a nap with me on the couch. I settle in, the weight of a cat next to me, when my phone rings.

Sigh. Can't a girl just take a nap with a fat cat in peace?

"Mia speaking."

"Mia. It's your mother."

The shock of hearing my mother's voice sends me shooting upright, Otis flying off the couch. Ice crackles through my veins, and heat scorched my skin at the same time. My stomach twists, and I can barely get out any words.

"Mom. Hi."

As I sit across from my parents in the Raven Diner, memories flood back unwanted, and I struggle to look them in the eye. These are the people who all but abandoned me, who had written me off.

The silence between us drags out, and I rack my brain for something to say. Anything.

Think, Mia. Think.

But my mother is quicker than I am, speaking first.

"You didn't let us know you are in town."

Not a question. An accusation.

"We hear you are investigating Lily's death all of a sudden. Like you care about what happened to your baby sister. Our sweet little girl."

My mother's words are like daggers in my heart, each plunged with precision to ensure maximum damage and pain.

I look up, trying to get the words out to defend myself, but they die in my throat as I watch my father put his arm around my mother. My mother, the perpetual victim, dabs the tears from her eyes, sniffling delicately.

"I don't understand where we went wrong with you, Mia."

The disappointment and disapproval in my father's voice are heavy, and the glare I receive to punctuate his words is a physical blow to my stomach.

Every single emotion I had felt during my childhood, every single time I had felt inferior, unloved, less than, unwanted, and unwelcome, washes through me like a tsunami, crushing on the shores of my will to live, drowning out any sense of belonging I had felt in the last few years thanks to Angie.

I sit back in my seat, my face as blank as I can make it, staring at my parents.

"Why are you back in town, Mom, Dad? You never kept in touch after Lily, so I am not sure why you want to now be in touch with me."

My mother sniffles again, dabbing more tears.

"We had to hear from strangers that you are here, looking into Lily's death, but you won't pick up the phone to let us know anything. We had been waiting so long to find out what happened to Lily, and...

what? You were just going to waltz into town, find what happened, and leave again, never telling us? I can't believe..."

My mother cuts herself off with a gasp, my father looking at her worriedly before he continues the thought on her behalf.

"You see what you are putting your mother through again? After the FBI dragged you away, we had to live with the shame of having a delinquent as a daughter. And now you cannot even let us know when you are finally doing something good by looking into Lily's murder. You should be ashamed of yourself, Mia. That is not how you treat family."

I almost want to laugh at the statement and how ridiculous it is. No, I think to myself, that is not how you treat family, but the example I had was not exactly the best, so I am not sure what they were expecting.

"I am here to investigate Lily's murder, yes, but I did not reach out as you abandoned me. You left me to the FBI and never kept in touch, even though I tried my best to. I was just a kid, and you wrote me off. I don't know what you were expecting from this conversation, but I am done with it. If I find who murdered Lily, I will make sure you are informed. I need to go now. I have work that requires my attention."

When I stand up, the shock on my parent's faces is almost comical. If it was not for the years of emotional abuse I had endured at their hands, I would be laughing.

Back at Ethan's house, I throw back a glass of whiskey. My nerves are shot after the conversation with my parents.

I need to keep myself busy until the tracker gives me something to work with.

I pop Ethan a text to hear if any fingerprints were pulled from the bible, knife, or note that was left at my door at the motel although I am sure there won't be any.

Feeling restless, I walk to my crime board, checking over all the details again and again.

My eyes land on Edgar Jones. The person who had landed me in trouble in the first place with his dare.

Taking his photo off the wall, I sit down at my laptop.

I actually don't know that much about Edgar, but maybe it's time I find out more.

A few hours of research later, I surfaced from the rabbit hole I just went down.

Edgar and his whole family have suspected ties to gangs in some or other capacity, and years have been spent trying to prove this. The Sampson Smugglers that Ethan had mentioned seem to be associates of some of these gangs, so they are not just friends of Edgar.

The Sampson Smugglers could be contracting to the Joneses to help move contraband of some sort and leaving it to the Joneses to kill off any loose ends.

The connection to the motel is still bothering me, though, and my mind keeps wandering to Adam.

He had been more than just shocked the day I booked in at the motel. He had been nervous.

I cast my mind back, the day feeling years away, and go through every detail.

His hand had been shaking, he had sweat beading on his forehead and upper lip, and he kept looking around furtively.

Perhaps I need to go push a few buttons and see if anything pops out.

I grab my phone and keys, give Otis a quick scratch, and lock the front door behind me.

Time for a quick talk with Adam.

# Chapter 15:

"Mia. You're back."

Adam's face drains of color as I walk to the reception desk of the motel. His right-hand reaches for something below the desk as he keeps his eyes on me.

"Hi, Adam. How are you doing today?" I say, trying to keep my voice light and friendly as I smile at him. "I'm not back to get a room, but I wanted to come over and chat with you. I realize we never got the chance to talk and catch up while I was staying here. How have you been?"

He frowns at me as I lean against the front desk, still smiling at him.

"I, uhm, yeah. I've been... I've been well. Working here and at the church most days. Being custodian of the church is a big responsibility," Adam says with condescension and suspicion as he frowns at me.

His right hand is still below the desk, where I cannot see it, and for a moment, I wonder if he has a concealed weapon. But that just seems ridiculous. This is Adam in front of me.

"Oh, I can imagine. I know you've got to regularly go lock and open the church for all the functions and events and make sure everything is clean and neat on top of that. How do you have enough time to work here at the motel as well?"

Adam's eyes narrow slightly as his frown deepens further. My line of questioning or the way I am framing the questions must be irking him.

"I have an arrangement with Father Donovan that makes it possible for me to work the reception here at the motel as well as look after the church. I'm happy to be of service to Father Donovan, ah, the church in whichever capacity."

My smile almost slips as he corrects himself about who he is of service to. Interesting. Very interesting... I need to see if I can find out more about Adam's connection with Father Donovan and his shift in allegiance from the church to the good priest.

"That's amazing, Adam. I am glad to hear you were able to make it work. It is truly great to see that you still enjoy being of service to the church after all these years. It was a highlight of my Sunday mornings to see you greeting everyone as they entered the church. It's a pity I never got to know Father Donovan much, though. He seems to be a good person, and the community likes him. Do you enjoy working with him here at the motel and the church?"

I keep my eyes on Adam as I ask the question to see if his face reveals anything concerning my line of questioning. The only change to his facial expression is the suspicion that flashes across his face before he replaces it with the slight frown he has had since I started talking to him.

"Father Donovan is a great man. I'm grateful to be working for him. The town is lucky to have him."

The clipped sentences indicate Adam's irritation with my line of questioning, but... Adam said, "for him," not "with him." Similar to his first slip, but this time, Adam didn't correct himself. Very interesting indeed.

"How good to hear. The town is indeed lucky to have someone like Father Donovan servicing the community and looking after their souls. I would love to get to know someone as amazing as Father Donovan better. He lives here in the motel, right?" Adam nods, and I continue. "If he is here, would you mind pointing me in his direction? It would be great to have a chat with him if he is available."

At this point, the frown on Adam's face seems to be a permanent scowl, but as he cannot seem to find anything strange in my questions, he clears his throat, looking at the time.

"Father Donovan should be here, yes. Room 21. But he is a busy man with a full calendar. He might not be available for an unscheduled meeting."

I smile inwardly at the admonishment from Adam about the "unscheduled meeting" as I thank him for the information and head off to find Father Donovan. Perhaps Father Donovan is somehow involved in all the accidents and ongoings in town and the surrounding towns.

Adam does not come across as a mastermind (he never has, to be honest), but the way he speaks of Father Donovan has me suspecting the good father of more than just shepherding his flock.

I need to find Father Donovan and connect the dots. I need answers.

As I knock on the door of Room 21, suspicions and questions run through my mind, along with possibilities of what I could find right here, right now.

Waiting for a reply to my knock, I realize I had never truly had a good look at Father Donovan except for photos in the local newspaper.

A muffled "Coming!" sounds from inside the room, and I hear some shuffling sounds before Father Donovan opens the door.

The surprise on his face as he sees who is in front of his door is quickly covered by a smile that I suppose is meant to be charming and inviting.

"You must be Mia Conrad, the FBI agent and a former resident of our little town. I heard you had been staying here in the motel with us for a while. Is there anything I can assist you with?"

He extends a hand to me in greeting, keeping the charming smile in place. But the mask-like setting of his face only succeeds in sending a chill down my spine.

"Father Donovan, it is good to meet you. And yes, I am Mia," I reply in a friendly voice, taking his offered hand. "I'm no longer staying at the motel, but no, there were no issues during my stay. I just wanted to meet you and chat with you for a while if you have the time. I haven't been in town for so many years, and I feel like I have missed out on a lot, especially when it comes to the church. And as I have heard that you are closely connected to so many people in town, I was hoping to spend some time with you, catching up on the happenings in the town and at the church."

Suspicion flickers in his eyes, but the friendly mask stays in place.

"Sure, I'd be happy to chat with you and catch you up on the church and the town. It would be my honor."

Smooth. And much more charming than any other Father I have dealt with.

"Thank you, Father, I would appreciate it. Would you like to go for a coffee while we chat, or would you prefer to talk here? I'm happy either way."

"A good cup of coffee is always welcome."

His smile widens into a more wolfish grin, and another chill runs down my spine.

This man is trouble.

With Father Donovan sitting across from me, I take my time to study him as the server takes his order and he flirts with her.

He had greeted every person as we walked in, lightly flirting with women and charming the men, not like any other priest I had met before. I had kept a slight smile on my face as everyone nodded to me in greeting, most likely only to look polite in front of Father Donovan as they had refused to greet me on previous occasions.

He is charming, that much is easy to see, but the way he handles himself reminds me more of a suave bachelor in the city than a priest. Not that priests should act only a certain way. They just, in general, care more about showing true concern for their church members than their hair or their looks. I have caught the good Father checking his hair in the car and the diner's window and checking to make sure that the women around him are indeed looking at him.

As the server leaves, Father Donovan returns his attention to me.

"Apologies, Mia. I like to stay connected to the town and people and enjoy greeting and speaking to everyone to make sure they know I am always available to them. Everyone in town has been so welcoming since I joined the church that it has been easy to care for not only the town but each person as an individual as well."

Smooth words and a smooth smile.

I return the good Father's smile as our coffees arrive.

"That is good to hear, Father. I am glad to hear you have found your space here in the community and that you are part of the town."

"Please, call me Donovan. 'Father' is much too formal in everyday conversations."

"Thank you, Donovan. I must say, you seem quite a bit younger than I had thought you would be. Is the small-town life not too boring or stifling for you?"

I need to get him to talk about himself, let his guard down, or give information that I can use to my advantage. From the moment I met him, something has been bothering me, and it is not only how charming and flirty he is. Something is lurking beneath the surface. Something dark.

"No, not at all," Father Donovan replies with a half laugh. "I found the city much too busy to my liking and was quite excited when I was called to Cedarwood. It wasn't much of an adjustment, either. Small-town life suits me."

"I see. And, if you don't mind me asking, which church were you preaching at before coming to Cedarwood? It must have been a much bigger congregation than you have here if you were preaching in the city."

A flicker of irritation crosses his eyes at my line of questioning, but the charming smile stays plastered to his mouth.

"I was preaching at a small church in Texas. It, unfortunately, closed just before I was called here due to a lack of funds. The calling to Cedarwood was heaven-sent, and I am thankful to be here every day."

Sipping my coffee, I nod in agreement, getting my next question ready. Father Donovan, sensing this, jumps ahead of me with a question of his own.

"Enough about me. How has it been for you to be back in town? I understand that you are looking into your sister's murder along with Detective Ethan Hayes. Have you made any progress?"

Ah, he is trying to divert the conversation. And why is he asking about Lily? Questions start running through my mind as I try to decipher his intent with the questions.

"It has been interesting to be back here. On the surface, it seems that not much has changed, but I see there have been improvements in town and a few new shops that opened, including this lovely place. And yes, I've been looking into Lily's death, but there is not much to find. It's sad, as I had hoped to help my family find some closure after all these years."

I hope my answer is enough to satisfy his curiosity, but I need to turn the conversation back to him.

"I am quite impressed with how the church has grown under your leadership, Donovan. I would love to hear more about it and catch up on what has been happening in town and at the church since I left Cedarwood."

Father Donovan flashes that charming smile at me again, leaning forward on the table as though he wants to speak to me in confidence.

"Sure, I'd love to share some stories with you. The church specifically has made some great strides over these last years. We now have support groups running for drug, alcohol, and gambling addiction, as well as family and trauma, counseling that anyone from Cedarwood and surrounding towns may attend."

That last bit about the groups… Anyone, including those from surrounding towns, may attend the groups: that is new information to me. Could this be the link I am looking for? I look down at my cup to keep any emotions crossing my face from giving my curiosity and overly intense interest away as I keep my fingers crossed that Father Donovan continues to elaborate on the church. Thankfully, he does.

"We also have an amazing youth group that volunteers at the retirement homes and animal shelters in the area, and I offer counseling to young people who feel the need to repent for their sins."

That turn of phrase... They come to him to repent for their sins, not share their burdens or ask for assistance. Yes, he might be a preacher, but "repent" is such a specific word... a very specific word used in those encrypted messages.

I smile at Father Donovan, doing my best to keep my eyes and face soft and kind and not to show any of the thoughts running through my mind. I need to dig further into the victims as soon as I can and see if any of them attended one or perhaps more of these groups at the church.

"The church seems like it is truly flourishing and serving the community and surrounds with your leadership, Donovan. I am impressed. Did you get counselors in for all the groups, or do you handle them yourself?"

I keep my voice casual, almost with a tone of distracted interest, as though I am simply being polite.

"No, it is not as much work as you would think. A counselor is not needed. I handle the group sessions and the private sessions myself. My time is the church's time. Adam is, of course, there to assist when needed, which does help me to serve the community better and gives me time for home visits where they are needed."

His charm tap seems to open on full now as he brushes his hair back while keeping his eyes on me. As he lifts his arm, a tattoo hidden underneath his shirt on the inside of his bicep catches my attention, pulling at the ghost of a memory. Where have I seen that tattoo before? It is gone too quickly for me to look at more closely as Father Donovan brings his arm back down, and I simply smile back at him, trying to be my kindest self and stuffing all my suspicions and wonderings to the back of my mind until I can get out of the café and back to my laptop.

"You are doing such great work for Cedarwood and the surrounding towns. I can understand why everyone seems to love your presence here and enjoy seeing you out and about, Donovan. I am glad the church community has you to lean on."

Still smiling, I wave down the server and request the bill.

"I hope you don't mind, but I saw the time, and I need to get back to work. This coffee is on me, though."

Father Donovan starts to protest, but I wave it off, handing the server money to cover the bill and tip.

"I enjoyed our conversation quite a bit. We must catch up later again, Mia."

Another chill skitters down my spine as his smile turns into a lupine grin that plays across his face in time with his words, but I keep my face calm, kind, and unbothered.

"We should do so, Donovan. Definitely."

Walking out of the café, I feel his eyes following me, piercing my back. As I reach the exit, I look up and see Father Donovan in the reflection of the glass door as he pulls out his phone to make a call. His eyes are still on my back, his smile gone.

I sent a message to Ethan and Kyle to meet me at Ethan's place after their respective workdays end. I need to tell them what I learned about the good Father today and get their thoughts. Father Donovan is linked to all of this and is a vital part of whatever conspiracy or organization is at work here. I know it. Now, I need to prove it.

I pull my laptop closer to start digging into Father Donovan, into Adam, into the support groups at the church. into the connections any of the victims might have had to the groups at the church and into Ray.

I need to dig into all of it.

Right now.

# Chapter 16:

I've found it. I've found the connection tying all the victims together.

All the victims had been to one of the support groups at the church. I've confirmed this thanks to online calendars, cellphone data, and the email accounts that I hacked over the last few hours.

My elation at this lasts only a few seconds, as I realize that Father Donovan is using the church against people trying to better themselves.

I need to find out more about Father Donovan.

On the surface, I have only been able to find details of his life in Cedarwood, as though his life started here. The church in Texas that he had mentioned over our coffee was a dead end as I could not find any churches that closed in the six months before Father Donovan had been called to Cedarwood.

Who is Father Donovan? And how is he recruiting people from the support groups?

I'll need assistance in answering these questions.

Where are Ethan and Kyle?

Ethan's thundercloud of a face as he walks into his house is a mirror to mine. The frustration of not finding more information on Father Donovan is getting to me. In a final bid to find more information, I have sent his photo to Angie to run against our database to see if there are any hits.

"Are you okay?" I ask Ethan as I look up from my laptop, hoping that the thundercloud face is not related to our case.

"He's gone. Ray seems to have disappeared without a trace. His cell phone and truck are at his house, but someone saw him get on a bus last night with a bag. No idea where he went. His bank account was also cleared out yesterday, according to Ronda. Your trace isn't going to work. We need a new plan to find out what is being smuggled."

I grind my teeth in anger. Ray has now screwed us over twice: first by not wanting to help, and now by running away. Bastard.

Closing my eyes and pinching the bridge of my nose between my thumb and forefinger, I rack my brain for a solution.

Maybe we could...

"You know, I think I have a plan that could work to help us figure out what these assholes are up to before someone else gets killed. But we will need Kyle's help, and he will need to be comfortable with lying. I will also need your help in kitting Kyle out with a listening device and a tracker. I'll handle the digital evidence needed to make this plan work. I just hope Kyle agrees to the plan once he hears how all the victims are connected and how they were most likely recruited."

Ethan's scowl turns into bewilderment at my explanation, or half explanation, and the comment about the connection between the victims and their recruitment.

"Uhm, Mia, what are you talking about? How will Kyle be able to help us prove anything?"

A knock on the front door interrupts my reply, and Ethan lets a happy-looking Kyle in.

"Hello, hello, people. How are you doing today?"

Ethan and I both frown at Kyle, and I see when the mood in the room sinks in for him.

"Ah, I see I walked into a very different mood than I just left at my mom's house."

"Everything okay with your mom?"

"Yeah, we just talked things out from the other day, and I understand her side and reasoning better now. I don't want to fight with her in any way. She and my sister are all that I have left."

I chew on the inside of my cheek as I realize my revelation about the connection between the victims might damage what Kyle had just rebuilt, but Ethan interrupts my thoughts, and a slight guilt and worry build in my chest.

"Glad to hear it, but we are having some trouble with the investigation. Ray disappeared last night; he took a bus. Mia has a plan for the investigation to continue without him. It has to do with the information she found on the connection between the victims and how they were chosen as recruits."

Kyle's smile fades as Ethan speaks, and he looks over to me.

"Oh, I see. Well, I am glad if there has been progress with the connection between the victims at least. What did you find, Mia?"

I sigh inwardly. This is not going to be an easy revelation for Kyle to hear about.

I think we all need a support drink.

"Let's grab something to drink first. There should be some white wine in the fridge still. Then we can sit and chat."

Both Ethan and Kyle have been looking at me expectantly for the last few minutes but say nothing as we pour the wine and each take a seat in the living room.

As the silence starts dragging, I take a sip of the wine and clear my throat. The best way to do this is to rip the band-aid off. Kyle will be okay.

"As I said in my message, I went to speak to Adam earlier today and then had a 'chat' with Father Donovan. As we spoke, I learned that the support groups at the church are open to people from surrounding towns as well and that Father Donovan acts as a counselor for all the different groups. This made me realize that every one of the victims that I have hacked so far had something to hide. Debt, addiction, assault, infidelity, gambling issues, and so on. Meaning, perhaps, they had gone to the good father and his groups for advice."

I stop for a moment to see Kyle's reaction to this, but there's only confusion on his face. He must not know the truth about his dad, or he doesn't want to...

"After I got home from coffee with Father Donovan, I dug deeper into all our victims and found that all of them had attended one or more of the support groups, and some of them had additional private sessions with Father Donovan as well. Kyle, your dad was in therapy for domestic abuse. Not because he was abused, but... because he was an abuser. From what I could find, your mom has been his only victim, the abuse contained in their marriage. I... I am sorry to be the one to tell you this. I know you care deeply about your dad and how much you miss him."

Kyle starts shaking his head even before I am done talking, staring down at his wine glass. I see the thoughts rushing through him, the immediate dismissal of my findings. My heart goes out to him, but I know I need to press on. We need to get to the bottom of the smuggling operation, and Kyle is pivotal to my plan.

"I know this is hard to hear, Kyle, but I found searches on your dad's internet history that indicate he had been trying to overturn that part of him for a long time. I am so sorry, and I understand you need a minute, but we do not have much time to put a plan into action to figure out what is being smuggled and who exactly is involved."

The silence in the room is heavy as I wait for Kyle to reply. I look to Ethan for assistance, but he is looking at Kyle with sympathy and something else I cannot identify. I wonder what Ethan's thinking about.

"She always said she just prefers long sleeves. And that she's clumsy. But she hasn't worn long sleeves in a while."

The pain in Kyle's voice has me wanting to reach a hand to him in sympathy, but I stop myself. This is something he needs to deal with if we want to get anywhere with my plan.

"Kyle, we need your help to continue this investigation. Your dad's actions towards your mom do not take away from what he did for you, what he meant to you. I understand that this is not easy to learn, but we need you. Will you be able to put your feelings aside for a moment and listen to Mia's plan? No matter what your dad did wrong, he did not deserve to be murdered."

I am unable to hide the look of shocked surprise that crosses my face at Ethan's words. That is the absolute last thing I would have expected him to say. I shake my head, trying to clear the surprise from my face before I turn to Kyle.

"Ethan's right, Kyle. Your dad did not deserve to be murdered, and we need you. Are you willing to listen to my plan and help us? Help us end this smuggling operation and the unnecessary deaths caused in Cedarwood and all the other towns. We can't do this without you, Kyle. Ethan and I need you."

Lifting his head up to look at me, I see the determination harden on Kyle's face.

"You're right. My dad was still my dad, and he did not deserve to be murdered, even though he undoubtedly deserved to be held accountable for what he did to my mom. What do you need me to do?"

It doesn't take me too long to explain my plan to Ethan and Kyle, but going over the finer details of what to do next and fabricating the evidence needed takes quite a while, and I yawn as I look at the time on my phone.

I look over the fabricated evidence on my laptop, feeling pleased with the results, and flick my eyes over my laptop to where Ethan and Kyle are busy with a variety of devices.

"This mic and its connected wire will need to be taped to your body under a loose-fitting shirt, and we will need to be within 500 feet of the device to pick up and record any audio. It will also be a good idea for you to wear pants with a belt that the battery pack of the device can be hooked onto. And you will need to ensure you do not stand with your back to Father Donovan, Adam, or anyone for that matter, so they do not see the battery pack by accident. This is a bit of an older and bulkier version, but it will do the job."

A slight smile steals onto my face as I see the concentration with which Kyle studies the device while listening to Ethan. That is the exact concentration Kyle used to have in school when playing football, and for some reason, the memory makes me want to smile.

Perhaps there are some good memories in this town for me after all.

"Mia, can you check the catch-all drawer in the kitchen for batteries? I need two double A's."

"Excuse me; you want me to check the what drawer?"

The look of embarrassment on Ethan's face and the little-boy grin he flashes me has a kaleidoscope of butterflies fluttering about in my stomach.

"Sorry. The bottom drawer is on the left-hand side of the kitchen. I chuck odds and ends in there."

Trying to shake off the butterflies, I turn to fetch the batteries and hear Ethan explaining the next device to Kyle: a button camera.

After a restless night's sleep and a day of impatient waiting, Ethan and I are sitting in Kyle's car near the church hall, waiting.

The fabricated evidence is in place for if and when it is needed, and Kyle has been kitted out with the wire and spy camera. I had installed a tracker on his phone as well, but I hope that there will be no need for it.

If anyone had to take a closer look at Kyle's car, they would be quite shocked to see Ethan and myself hanging low in the backseat of Ethan's car. The receiver for the mic and my laptop is between us, with the video feed from the button camera running on the laptop screen. A pair of earphones is connected to the laptop for us to listen to the conversation on the other end of the devices.

"I hope Kyle will stay calm and hook Father Donovan as we discussed."

Ethan looks at me over the devices between us.

"He'll be fine. He wants to get to the bottom of this as much as we do. We'll get the answers we need. One way or another."

I nod my head, more to myself than Ethan. So much of the plan hinges on how this meeting goes and how Kyle handles himself. This has to work. It has to.

Voices start greeting each other on the other end of the mic as people come into sight on the camera feed. Ethan and I each grab an earphone to listen, my nerves hitting harder.

Father Donovan opens the group with a greeting and a prayer, and each of the attendees introduces themselves stating why they are there, including Kyle with a vague allusion as to why he is participating in the group. So far so good.

Ethan and I listen intently as the group session kicks off in earnest and Father Donovan gives advice and encouragement to the various sharers in the group. As the group gets to Kyle, he does exactly as we asked.

"Father Donovan, I am not sure I can share tonight. It is all much too raw, and I feel as though I won't be able to share outside of a private conversation yet. I hope that's okay. Just being here and hearing from everyone is already helping me. I hope to soon have the same courage to speak about my struggles."

"Of course, Kyle, of course. We will talk after the group session. I am sure there is a way that I can help lighten your burden."

I silently high-fived Ethan at these words from Father Donovan. Kyle did exactly as we had discussed, and now the good Father wants to speak to him alone. Perfect.

The rest of the session had dragged on for ages (or it at least felt so, sitting in the car, waiting) with quite a few more people sharing and Father Donovan giving more advice and more encouragement. Finally, though, Kyle is alone with Father Donovan in his office next to the church, and Ethan and I perk up to hear if our plan, our trap has worked.

"So, Kyle, what is it that I can help you with? You seem truly troubled."

Kyle's sigh over the mic is authentic and sounds somewhat hopeless. He is truly leaning into the role we created for him.

"Father, I'm in over my head. I... I got into some financial trouble, well, gambling trouble to be honest, a while ago, and... And now... Now I am afraid I might lose my practice, my house, my mom's house, everything. I have mountains of debt, and I don't know what to do. And the creditors are coming after me. I don't know how long I have before it all gets out of control... until they come for me."

There are a few moments of silence on the other side before Father Donovan replies.

"All hope is never lost, Kyle. I can help you. To repent your sins and get out of debt. Wipe the slate clean and give you a chance to start over, start fresh."

My excitement at Father Donovan's words is reflected in Ethan's face as we look at each other in the dark car, our faces lit only by the feeble light from the laptop screen.

"Kyle, what would you be willing to do to repent your sins and get rid of your debt? Would you be willing to perform a single task, no questions asked?"

Father Donovan's voice is low and soothing, convincing. His eyes look intense and hypnotic via the camera feed as he leans forward towards Kyle, watching Kyle's face intently, waiting for an answer.

"Is that even possible, Father? If it is, then yes. I would do anything."

Father Donovan sits back with a satisfied smile on his face.

"Good. Very good. Do not worry about this further. Go home, rest, and wait for my message. You will know it when you see it. The key that you will need to understand all of this can be found on the announcement board in the church. Make sure no one sees you when you go look for it. We wouldn't want anyone to find out about your little secret, now, would we?"

The same lupine grin that had been thrown towards me yesterday at the end of my conversation with the good father plays across his face as he utters those last words to Kyle.

A monster: that is what he is.
A wolf in shepherd's clothing.
But our plan worked.
We will get our wolf.

# Chapter 17:

Keeping myself busy for two days has not been easy. Ethan and Kyle both have work to focus on daily, but with all the information that I could uncover gathered, sorted, and filed within one day, I happily jump for my phone when Angie's name appears on the caller ID.

"Hi, Angie! I'm so glad you called!"

My enthusiasm might be a bit over the top but having spent the whole morning doing laundry and cleaning around me, I need something new to distract me from the waiting.

"Hi, Mia. You sound, ah, excited. Everything okay there?"

I give Angie a quick rundown of what had happened over the last three days since I spoke to her and the waiting game I am playing at present. Her silence on the other end of the line has me checking my phone screen to see if the line dropped. Perhaps she needs time to process.

After a few more moments of silence, Angie finally sighs before she answers me.

"In light of what you told me now and from what I found, I think you might be sitting on a massive case and dealing with some extremely dangerous people, Mia. I ran the photo you sent me, and the results I got back are... confusing. Are you close to your laptop?"

I walk to my laptop, turn it on, and confirm the same with Angie.

"I'm sending you a file now with what I found. Father Donovan Brown did not exist before he was called to Cedarwood. The records and details for him seem to have suddenly sprung to life roughly four weeks before he was offered the position at the church, with nothing that I could find from before that. Stranger than this, though, I could not pick up any names or aliases for the individual in the photo that you sent. It is as though he didn't exist until Cedarwood. The only connection I could find is that this individual has been photographed in San Antonio and New York meeting with suspected and convicted smugglers, money launderers, and drug dealers."

I wait impatiently for the file to come through on my email so that I can see the photos Angie is referring to. Who is this man? And how did he end up in Cedarwood, pretending to be a preacher?

"I have the file open in front of me, Angie. You're right, this is extremely strange. We should definitely be able to pick up at least an alias, if not a name."

As I scroll down through the file, I get to the photos of Father Donovan, or whoever the hell he is, meeting with various parties. Each photo only shows him meeting with one or more people, nothing incriminating.

Wait. There.

I go back to the fourth photo.

That is Adam and Edgar Jones with Father Donovan in Dallas, six weeks before Father Donovan was called to Cedarwood. And these other people in the photo... Those are two of the members of the Sampson Smugglers to whom Edgar Jones allegedly has ties to. But that third person... his neck tattoo looks familiar. If only I could remember from where or why.

"Mia, what do you see? Usually, when you go quiet like that, you have found something."

I smile at how well Angie knows me, even when we are miles and miles apart, and share what I found in the photo with her.

"That is indeed interesting. So, Adam and Edgar both met with Father Donovan before Father Donovan existed or was called to Cedarwood."

"They might have been part of the plan to get him here, to integrate him into the church community. It would make sense, as Adam knew the old preacher was retiring, and a replacement would be needed quite some time in advance."

I chew on this information for a while, and I can hear Angie also thinking and turning the information over on the other end of the phone.

"I wish there were a quick answer here, but I think you will need to follow through with the plan you, Ethan, and Kyle have to gather additional information on what is going on in Cedarwood and the surrounding towns and to find who murdered Lily. But I am beginning to suspect she saw or heard something she shouldn't have and was disposed of because of this."

"I agree with you. The evidence we have gathered so far points to Lily being in the wrong place at the wrong time and being killed for that. I might not have all the details yet, but I do know, in my gut, that Father Donovan and Adam are somehow involved in her murder. They are responsible, even if they were not the ones who strangled her."

My phone pinging in my ear has me distracted, and I pull it away from my face to check who the text message is from.

It's Kyle, and his message is only two words long.

*It's on.*

Thirty minutes hasn't felt this long in a while as I pace up and down in the living room, waiting for Ethan and Kyle to get here.

Otis is on the couch, watching and keeping me company, looking not too pleased with my pacing but happy for the scratches every now and then.

A car door closing outside the house has me bolting for the front door and yanking it open just as Ethan opens it from outside, and I stumble right into him.

I look up at him in surprise, blood flooding my cheeks as I see my expression reflected on his face.

Before either of us can say anything, Kyle pulls up, almost having to make an emergency stop in his haste to not overshoot Ethan's house.

I stand aside to let Ethan inside as Kyle hurries up the driveway, throwing worried glances at the surrounding houses, his nervousness clearly visible on his face.

I hear the kettle in the kitchen as Kyle steps inside the house, and I close the door behind him.

Heading to the living room, Kyle and I sit down, and Ethan follows with French press coffee and a mug for each of us.

"Good. Fuel. We are going to need it," Kyle remarks as he looks at the coffee.

Taking a hard look at Kyle, I see the jittery hands clamped over his phone and his slightly wild, unseeing eyes. We need to keep him calm for the next few days, or this investigation will fail.

I look to Ethan to see if he has noticed Kyle's nerves, but he is busy with the coffee.

"Kyle, I think you should put your phone down for a few moments," I remark casually. "Let's have some coffee and discuss the next steps to make sure we're all on the same page."

His head whips up to me much too quickly, Kyle looks from me to the phone he is clutching, relaxing his death grip on the phone and sitting back in the chair.

I wait for Ethan to hand out the coffee and take a seat before I continue.

"Now that Kyle has received the message, I will confirm that it was posted on the same notice board that the other messages had been posted and check that the message is the same."

I look between Ethan and Kyle as I speak but shift my attention to Kyle in full, waiting to make sure he is looking at me before I continue.

"But Kyle, you'll still need to go to the church noticeboard. Father Donovan is most probably keeping an eye out to make sure that you go to the board to find 'the key' as instructed, so you need to pretend as though you're searching for it. You cannot just walk to whatever thing is on the board that points you in the direction of the Day of the Dead or the University of Toronto or anything related to this. Pretend to check your phone and the message you received, and then read on the board. Do this a few times and remember to frown and look somewhat lost and worried. A few glances over your shoulder while you're in front of the board won't hurt either, as the good Father will think that you are heeding his threat."

Kyle keeps nodding as I speak, although I am not sure how much he has taken in. Ethan keeps quiet, listening to my instructions for Kyle, as he slowly sips his coffee.

"It is vitally important that Father Donovan continues to believe this ruse. I've received some information about Father Donovan, Adam, and Edgar from my boss, and we need to be careful. There is more going on here than we know or have found so far. Angie sent me information on Father Donovan after I asked her to run his photo and name against the FBI's databases."

Ethan sits up at my words, focusing his full attention on me.

"What did Angie send to you?"

Wow. I had only mentioned Angie's name once or twice in front of Ethan, and he remembered it. With that kind of information retention, it is no wonder he is such a good detective.

I quickly gave them a rundown of the information Angie sent to me earlier and who I had found in the pictures that were included in the file. Both Ethan and Kyle's eyebrows lift in surprise as I mention the meeting photo from Dallas and all the players that had been at the meeting.

"You're right, Mia. We need to be extremely careful as we continue with the investigation. Kyle, if you feel uncomfortable continuing with the collection and effectively being bait for the investigation, you need to tell us now. We're not going to put you in any type of danger that you're not comfortable dealing with. And I will not be sending you to the collection unarmed. I have my private firearm that I'll give to you to keep with you in your car. Mia will also be armed. I just wish I could go as well without arousing suspicion, but if both Mia and I are suddenly not in town on the day that you are away, we might encounter issues with the good Father becoming suspicious."

The three of us sit in silence as Ethan and I wait for Kyle to process the information and the offer of a firearm for self-defense and protection.

I struggle to read Kyle's face and thoughts as the silence continues to stretch out, and I look to Ethan to see if there is anything that I can read in his face, but his concentration is wholly focused on Kyle. The frown between his eyes is seemingly etched there permanently, and his eyes are intensely brooding.

"No. No, I need to do this. I want to do this. I realize the danger, and I understand that many things can go wrong, but all the victims were left alive to make the collection and delivery and were only murdered two weeks later. I can do this and make sure we get the information we need. I want to get these assholes for killing Lily, my father, and all the other victims. The accident victims might have all had something that they were hiding, but Lily was blameless, innocent. She did *not* deserve to be killed, and it is my fault she went to Father Donovan that day in the first place. I... Mia, I am so sorry for keeping the truth about Lily and my relationship from you in the beginning and for being the reason Lily was murdered. I honestly loved her and wanted to build a life with her. I was... I was young, selfish, and stupid and could only see the fun in front of me and I didn't take how she felt into consideration. Can you forgive me?"

The sudden change of topic catches me off guard, and I stare at Kyle, frowning.

"Kyle," I slowly say, "my forgiveness should not matter, but if it will help you, I do forgive you. I know you weren't trying to keep information from me on purpose in the beginning, and it's not your fault Lily was murdered. It takes two to tango, Lily made her own decisions. And your hands were not the hands that ended her life. You are doing everything you can to help bring justice to her and all the other victims. You do not need to feel any further guilt."

The palpable relief on Kyle's face leaves me wondering how long he had been holding onto those words, but I shift the thoughts to the back of my mind. We need to strategize the next steps and make sure we have everything in place.

We only get one chance to get the information and evidence we need. There will be no second chances.

"Give me your phone and let me check the noticeboard and message so that we can get this show on the road. We only have two days to make sure this goes off without a hitch. Ethan, do you have any other toys that we can make use of to ensure we get the evidence we need?"

I have never been good at sitting around, waiting for time to pass, but we must wait the two days as specified before Kyle can go collect the package, whatever it is.

MasterOfAll had indeed been the one to post the message again, and it had been the exact same message as before with identical instructions. Kyle had found the reference to the paper about Mexico on the church noticeboard as part of an advertisement for holiday packages in Mexico. The flyer looked fake, and the company that posted it turned out to be a shelf company registered in the Cayman Islands. Anyone who tried to search for the company online would get to the website's homepage only to find that nothing on the site works.

My guess is that Father Donovan and his friends will be using the company in the future to funnel some of their business through. The stacks of cash Ethan and I saw in the barn on the Jones farm need to be going somewhere, and if that somewhere is no longer safe, a shelf company is the perfect way to funnel it.

I have packed and repacked my bag and the items I plan to take with me when I follow Kyle to New York Harbor, but I start getting on my own nerves.

Firmly zipping the bag closed, I turn around and head to the living room to watch a movie, determined to divert my attention. Hopefully, a good movie and cuddling a chunky cat will keep me busy for the rest of the evening and allow me to sleep through the night.

We need to make an early start tomorrow morning.

# Chapter 18:

The trip to New York Harbor is smooth, and Kyle seems to be calm and collected for the most part. Of course, he still needs to play the part of a scared and somewhat unwilling participant when he reaches the harbor, but I know that he will be able to handle it.

Ethan and I had spent a lot of time with Kyle the last two days going over every single detail of our plan, making sure he knew what to look out for at the harbor and when he should pull back and remove himself from any possible danger.

Kyle has been driving with a hidden camera in his dash, as well as the button camera on his shirt again, and I had activated it to record to a device hidden in his car. The device is set up to relay all recordings to cloud storage as well. It is a nifty little piece of equipment I have used on previous occasions that arrived via courier from Angie yesterday.

I owe her a massive bunch of flowers as soon as I get home.

Kyle arrives at the harbor about an hour after me. His instructions had said he needed to take backroads, and we had worked out a route that would take only an hour longer than the usual highways. With me arriving first, it allowed me to set up my long lens camera and find a good vantage point from which I can see exactly where Kyle goes and with whom he meets. My rangefinder binoculars are also with me, and I use them to keep an eye on Kyle's vehicle.

The instructions gave no details as to where Kyle needs to go when he reaches the harbor, but as he pulls up to the entrance, a man in black overalls walks to his car. The man knocks on the passenger side window, indicating to Kyle to open the door.

The man gets into Kyle's car and directs him to a building not far from the entrance of the harbor. He gives instructions on how he should park his car, with the trunk of the car pointing at a specific angle.

I swap the binoculars for my camera and start snapping pictures of the building exterior, the angle at which Kyle had to park, the man in the overalls, everything.

Indicating for him to stay in the car and pop the trunk, the man gets out, walks into the building, and comes back out carrying two large duffle bags. These he does not put in the trunk, though, but on the back seat of Kyle's car.

As the man places the two duffle bags on the back seat, another man in black overalls walks out of the building carrying a much larger bag in both arms. The bag seems to be moving as he places it in the trunk of the car, being much gentler than anyone would be with a duffle bag in general.

Frowning at this turn of events, I plug my earphones into my phone and check if I can stream the button camera recording. The audio will be delayed compared to what I see through my camera lens, but it will give me a better idea of what is going on.

The camera recording starts playing, and I hear the first man in overalls explaining to Kyle that he needs to wait; there is one more bag that needs to be added to the items.

The fourth bag is much smaller than the others and carried out by a third man in overall pants and a tank top. The bag is about half the size of the duffle bags on the backseat and a quarter of the size of the duffle bag in the trunk but seems sturdier somehow.

My frown deepens as I study the third man who walked out and the tattoo he has on his neck. That tattoo... It is the same one that the unknown person in the photo with Father Donovan and Adam had. Then it hits me: it's the same tattoo that Father Donovan has on the inside of his bicep. The same tattoo. I have seen it somewhere else as well, though.

Think, Mia.

Think.

I shake my head, shifting my attention back to Kyle and the instructions the man in the tank top is giving him.

"Drive straight back to the delivery point using back roads like you did on the way here. Do not open the duffle bags. We'll know if you did, and you don't want to find out what will happen then. We know where you live, where you work, where you eat, and who your family is. Only stop for fuel, nothing else. And do not get stopped by the cops. Got it?"

Kyle nods at the man, confirming his agreement, and turns his car to head back to the gate.

I keep my eyes on the building as the three men continue talking outside. The one in the tank top is clearly in charge as he gives some or other type of instruction to the other two, and they walk inside the building. Tank Top pulls out and lights a cigarette, checking his surroundings.

He continues to drag on the cigarette for a few minutes, giving me the chance to take a few good shots of his face and tattoo.

He flicks the cigarette butt away and stalks inside.

The journey back is much longer, as this time, I need to stay behind Kyle, ensuring a good distance between our vehicles in case there are any eyes or ears around reporting Kyle or my movements back to Father Donovan or any of the other parties possibly involved in this organization.

Kyle stops only once for fuel and to phone me.

He keeps hearing muffled noises coming from the trunk of his car, and I know that the wriggling duffle bag does not contain just some random item; there is a person in that bag.

Convincing Kyle not to open the bag takes all my strength, as I know how he feels. I also want to help, but we need to catch the receivers unloading the smuggled items, even if that does include a human.

The rest of the way feels extra-long, knowing that a person's life is in jeopardy, but we knew going into this that it would not be easy uncovering the smuggling operation or proving who is involved with it.

Kyle finally arrives at the Jones farm and turns onto the dirt road much more gently than I know he usually would have, his mind on the person in his trunk.

I park my car across the road, some distance away, and I jog over the road to the barns where I know the items will be offloaded. My smaller camera will need to be used for this part of the operation, as I cannot lug the long lens with me. I can neither run with it nor be inconspicuous at a short distance.

I reach the tree line near the barns just as Edgar walks out to Kyle, greeting him with a wolfish grin.

Kyle makes to get out of his car, but Edgar shuts the door on him, showing that he needs to stay in the car. I can only hear a word here and there, but I take as many photos as possible.

The two men I had seen counting money with Edgar walk out of the furthest barn and start taking the duffle bags from the back seat. Edgar himself walks to the trunk and lifts out the largest duffle bag, the one with the person in it. The movements seem feebler than before. Whoever is in the bag must be exhausted and suffering from the heat and lack of oxygen and water. My disgust runs deep at this, and I have to concentrate hard to not immediately walk out of my hiding place and simply shoot Edgar.

We need evidence. I am here to gather proof of what is going on in the town so that we can stop the killings and solve Lily's murder. I keep repeating this to myself as Edgar walks into the barn with the duffle bag and comes back out to show Kyle he needs to leave.

As Kyle drives past my hiding place, I see the disgust and anger on his face. I wish I could tell him that we will get these bastards, but I have work to do. Sneaking around the back of the barns as quietly as possible, I make my way to the furthest barn to get a closer look at what the items in the duffle bags are. There is a small gap between two planks at the back of the barn that gives me some view of what is going on inside the barn, and I line my camera lens up with the gap.

The largest duffle bag is on the table where the money is being counted, and Edgar goes over to zip it open calling to the other men.

"Boys let's see what we got this time. Hopefully, this one is more willing than the previous packages."

The men laugh crudely in agreement with his comment, walking closer to see who is in the bag.

A young girl, no older than seventeen, half-conscious and scared out of her mind, is pulled from the bag.

Her hair and clothes are dirty, and her wrists and feet are tied with zip ties. There is duct tape over her mouth, and a cattle ear tag is stuck through her right ear: right through it, like some sort of grotesque piercing.

I want to vomit, but I force my meal to stay inside my body as I continue to take photos.

"Nice, much prettier than the previous one. I get the first round to try her out. Then she's all yours. But first, take her downstairs. We need to unpack the shipment before the boss gets here."

"Nah, Edgar, man, you always take the prettiest ones for yourself. Give us a chance as well," sneers one of the men as he smirks and grabs the girl, hoisting her over his shoulder. Her muffled screams through the duct tape are gut-wrenching, and I focus on the fact that we will be getting her out soon.

If not tonight, tomorrow. But we *will* get her out.

It takes Edgar and his men about 30 minutes to unpack the other three duffle bags onto the table. The smaller bag contains what seems to be about 15kgs or 20kgs of cocaine. The two smaller bags are filled with stacks of dollar bills.

Just as Edgar and his men pull out two bill counters, a car drives up the farm road.

Looking up at the sound, Edgar notes to the men, "Boss is here. No funny business. You know what happened to the previous guys that decided to be funny with the boss."

Edgar's men look at each other, worry flashing across their faces as they get up to greet the boss.

"Mister Jono, good to see you again."

"I told you to call me Donovan in front of the help, Edgar. You are not as indispensable as you think. I can easily replace you with someone else more... qualified for the job. It gets tedious having to get rid of the help every time you slip up. The organization can only send replacements so often."

Chills run down my spine, and the knot in my stomach becomes a boulder sitting on my chest.

I knew he was pretending, but to hear the coldness and hate in his voice was something else entirely.

I continue taking pictures as Father Donovan walks into the barn.

Only this is not the Father Donovan anyone in town has ever seen.

A tight, sleeveless shirt has his tattoo on full display, and the evil sneer on his face is enough to give any rational person nightmares.

And I know, I know in my heart: this is my sister's murderer. This is the person who squeezed the life out of Lily.

This is the person who enjoyed watching the life drain from her eyes as her last breath left her body.

This is the person who could care so little that he stuffed her body in a freezer to deal with later.

This is the person I am going to kill.

# Chapter 19:

Focus.

Focus.

Focus, Mia, FOCUS.

*FOCUS!*

The hate building up inside of me is unlike anything I have ever felt. Washing away all sense of self-preservation, replacing it with an unending urge to ensure I get revenge. Right here. Right now.

A roaring in my ears, like a screaming voice telling me to take everything from the monsters in front of me.

The struggle to keep my concentration on the task of taking photos is a battle that I am about to lose.

And I don't care.

Fuck focus.

My sister might not have been good to me or cared about me, but no one, not one single person, deserves to die as she did.

The other victims all had their issues and darkness within them as well, but instead of giving them a chance to come clean, be better, try harder, or be brought to justice, they were killed off.

I put the camera down on the ground next to me, slowly, carefully, pulling the gun Ethan gave me earlier from my belt. Justice will need to wait for another day.

Today. Today, I want to make sure revenge reigns.

I will make sure it does.

Father Donovan, Jono, whoever the fuck he might be, will not be walking away from this.

I get up noiselessly, keeping my eye on the scene inside the barn before I turn to my right to go around the barn. To shoot him, Edgar, and the two assholes working with them.

To get that girl out and away and back to her family.

Only to be stopped dead in my tracks by Ethan coming towards me, walking softly and carefully, keeping as quiet as possible.

The shock on his face at my facial expression and the gun would be comical in almost any other situation. But it is exactly what I need to shake me out of my revenge haze.

I close my eyes, shaking my head, willing my heart into a slower rhythm.

My hands shake slightly as I put the safety on and stuff the gun back in my belt, indicating to Ethan to join me at the back of the barn where the activity inside it can be viewed.

I pick the camera back up and point it at the scene inside the barn, wishing for all the world that it was a sniper rifle and not just a camera.

Ethan squats down beside me as the roaring in my ears starts to subside, and I can hear the conversation in the barn again.

A nudge on my arm has me looking at Ethan and the cell phone he holds out to me, opened to a digital notepad.

*Mia, what did you see?*

No judgment, only a simple question.

As I look up at his face, I see that there is nothing but concern and care in his face. Not a hint of anger or admonishment to be seen.

I balance the camera on one knee, taking Ethan's phone to reply.

But how do I reply?

How do I explain what I just experienced after seeing them haul off that poor girl, bound and gagged, crying? How do I describe what went through my mind when I witnessed Father Donovan as his true self?

I stare at the cell phone screen, unseeing, as I hear Father Donovan's voice drifting to me from inside of the barn.

"I assume you put the live cattle downstairs. Is she anything to look at?"

Edgar and the other two snicker at this comment, and the roaring in my ears threatens to drown out everything again.

Deep breath in and out.

Focus, Mia.

Focus.

*They have a girl downstairs. She's bound. The money and drugs are on the table. Edgar and the other two were getting ready to count the money when Father Donovan showed up. Why are you here?*

As I hand the cell phone back to Ethan, I look back up, shifting my focus to the scene in the barn.

Edgar and the other two are moving the stacks of cash to count using the equipment they brought out while Father Donovan is checking the cocaine.

"Perhaps I should go see our new friend and make sure she has all the *amenities* she needs," Father Donovan says. The way his voice is a sickly caress on the word "amenities" has my heart dropping into my stomach, nausea gripping my whole body. "Give me the keys to the storage room."

The storage room? They call the place where they keep the women a storage room. These men are sick. And I need to stop them. Right now.

The roaring in my ears increases, and my rage builds up, blinding me. Again.

Ethan's hand on my arm brings me back to reality as he sees the look on my face. And I know he also heard what was happening in the barn by the thunderclouds building in his eyes.

Instead of handing me his cell phone, Ethan shows me the screen.

*I know we need to go in. Need to be smart about it. Lure some of them out. Then take out rest. Got zip ties for extra cuffs. Let's move away and plan.*

I nod to Ethan, and we move away silently.

To plan.

To take them down.

To get revenge.

Ethan and I know exactly what needs to be done as we split up, leaving the cover of the trees behind the barn. Weapons in hand. Plans laid out.

Even though Ethan was supposed to wait in town, I am glad he decided to show up here to back me up, armed to the teeth with some of his extra toys in tow.

As I move around the barn to the open door, Ethan takes up position close to the stack of hay bales a few steps across from the barn entrance.

With Ethan in position, I pull the pin on the smoke grenade and toss it into the barn: right onto the table between Edgar and the two scumbags helping him count the money.

The shouts and screams, interlaced with coughs from inside the barn, start moving toward the door, and I get ready to take down the first person to emerge. The second will be Ethan's problem, and the third is up for grabs.

Adam is the first to emerge, spluttering and coughing, eyes streaming with tears. I grab his arm, swinging him to my side as I kick his feet from under him. I cuff him with some of the zip ties Ethan provided, securing his hands and feet and duct-taping his mouth, as I hear Ethan fire a shot.

I jump back up, and I see Edgar down on the ground, holding his bleeding leg. I grab him by the collar and haul him away from the barn entrance, cuffing and gagging him as well.

With only one more man still to emerge, Ethan starts moving closer to the barn, to me, as I peer around the side of the door, trying to see through the clearing smoke. The man has a gun in hand but is still blinded by the smoke, coughing as he moves around the table. The wildly swinging gun in his hand makes it difficult to approach him, and I signal to Ethan to check from the other side of the barn if he has a clean shot.

As Ethan moves to check inside the barn, the man decides to take a few shots towards the door, forcing both Ethan and me to take cover.

Still coughing and firing at random, the man emerges from the barn, blinking away his tears in the sun.

Ethan and I lock eyes for a moment, and I nod to him in understanding as he holsters his gun.

I duck low, running for the man's legs at the same moment that Ethan launches his hands for the gun. We hit him from two sides, taking him down. While I zip-tie and gag him, Ethan disarms the gun, tossing the pieces in different directions.

As I turn back to Ethan, a gunshot goes off. Ethan doesn't make a sound, only suddenly clutches his side. Blood spreads across his shirt and leaks from beneath his hands.

Shock freezes me in place for a moment before my training kicks in, and I dive to the left to take cover behind the barn door. A second shot goes off as I move, hitting where I was squatting moments before next to the man in the dirt.

"Mia, run. Go," Ethan grunt-screams at me, still clutching his side, trying to move out of the barn door opening to find cover.

"Shut up, you fucking pig," Father Donovan swears, hitting Ethan in the head with the butt of his gun and opening a gash on Ethan's brow. "Stay right there on the ground, Detective, and Mia, sweetheart, why don't you kick your gun away and come join me? I'd be careful if I were you and not try anything rash. I am not sure your boyfriend over here would be able to survive any additional holes in his body. It seems like he's already bleeding quite a bit here."

I glare at Father Donovan as he grins at me, and, keeping my eyes on him, I put the gun on the ground. As I get up slowly, I kick the gun away, still holding his stare.

"See that, pig, she actually cares enough about you to give herself up," he says with a laugh, kicking Ethan in the ribs.

My thoughts race as I try to see a way out of the situation without getting Ethan killed or myself shot. I still have zip ties, duct tape, a flare, and a knife hidden in my shoe. None of these will work at a distance; I need to get close to Father Donovan. Men like him do not respond well to threats, but perhaps if I am able to make him believe...

I soften my glare somewhat and avert my gaze, slumping my shoulders a bit.

"Please don't hurt Ethan anymore. I... I'll do what you want; we'll both cooperate." I stutter over the words, hoping that my victim-playing will work.

Father Donovan grins at me, clearly taking my averted gaze, slumping shoulders, and slightly quivering voice as a sign of defeat.

"Wonderful. Let's all be friends. Mia, why don't you come and grab Ethan over here, help him up, and let's go talk inside? The boys can wait a bit to be untied. I think they have disappointed me enough for one day. A bit of time to repent their sins is exactly what they need before I deal with them later."

I move over to Ethan, Father Donovan keeping his gun pointed at Ethan to keep me in line. I gently take Ethan by the arm on his uninjured side to help him up. He groans as we stand up, the blood still flowing from his side, the stain spreading down to his pants.

I try to reason with Father Donovan. "We need to bind his wound. He is going to bleed out. And a cop's death on your hands would be bad for business. Please, let me help him." Keeping my voice scared and wobbly, my eyes on Ethan, I hope that Father Donovan will say yes if I pretend to cooperate and submit to him.

His answering snicker is anything but kind as he shoves me in the back. "We'll patch your boyfriend up in a while, but let's first talk for a bit. I am interested to hear how you two lovebirds found my little operation. Let's move this party downstairs," he remarks with a smile, seeming almost friendly, as he indicates to the stairs that lead below the barn. "Just down the stairs there. And make sure that he doesn't bleed on my money and products as we move through the barn and the space below. It will not help to improve my current mood after you interrupted my private time with my other guest."

I let Ethan lean against me as much as is needed while I fight the nausea at Father Donovan's implication of his other guest. Ethan's face is drawn and sallow as he tries to keep pressure on the wound while we shuffle forward. The pain must be excruciating, and I do my best to help him alleviate it as much as possible.

Making our way down the stairs is not going to be easy as the space is cramped.

"Ethan, you are going to have to lean on me from behind to get down the stairs. We'll need to work together. Just... Just take it slow."

"Now, now, Mia. Don't get all emotional on me and dawdle. Get moving."

Father Donovan shoves Ethan towards me from behind with his gun, causing Ethan to stumble as pain ripples across his face. I catch Ethan, holding him as gently as possible, while I grimace at his full weight hanging on me.

"I am tiring of this shit, Mia. Get him moving down those stairs," Father Donovan drawls. He sounds bored, as though holding an FBI agent and a wounded cop at gunpoint is an everyday occurrence for him.

"We're moving," I say as I release Ethan and turn to take the first step down the stairs, Ethan's hands on my shoulders.

We move down the stairs in tandem, going slow. Ethan's breathing is uneven, labored from pain, while we inch down, step by step. As we reach the bottom of the stairs, Ethan sags against me, whispering my name and a few other unintelligible words.

I turn to Ethan, trying to keep him upright, but he slides to the floor as Father Donovan steps into the basement space.

"Oh dear. It seems your boyfriend is in a bit of a pickle here. Why don't we get him up on a crate so that you and I can chat a bit."

I pull Ethan up again and move to help him onto the nearest crate, but a not-so-gentle kick to my backside from Father Donovan has me pausing in my tracks.

"Not the wooden crate, Mia. Think. I won't be able to get the blood out of the wood grain. Use the steel crate to prop our friend up on. Much easier to hose off after he is done leaking onto my stock. Or if he decides to expire there, it will be much easier to move him. See? The crate has little wheels. So convenient."

Working hard to keep the disgust and anger from my face, working to play the role of a scared and subservient woman, I help Ethan onto the steel crate. I try to make him as comfortable as possible, but the pain on his face tells me that there is nothing, absolutely nothing, I can do to help him here. Not without the assistance of medical personnel and equipment.

I turn back to Father Donovan, keeping my face in the mask of what I know he would like to see most: fear and obedience.

"What now, Father Donovan? What is all of this?" I ask as I gesture to the crates, the basement space, and the barn. I hope he will think the wobble in my voice is from fear and not the raging anger burning a hole in my stomach. "And why Cedarwood and the surrounding towns? I am sure there are other places that you would be able to operate from in complete anonymity. Where your victims and operations would not stand out. Where no one would be able to see the patterns."

Father Donovan smiles, his grin turning lupine again. The grin of a hunter, a murderer.

# Chapter 20:

I need to keep him talking and get him comfortable.

Get as much information from him.

And then I need to get close to him.

While I make sure he thinks he is in control.

A sudden, loud noise to my left has me jumping, and Father Donovan sighs dramatically at the noise. Ever the calm and benevolent man in any situation.

"It seems my other guest is feeling a bit left out. Give me a moment to check on her, won't you? I wouldn't want her pretty little feet to get damaged when I can make quite a few bucks from them before she goes to her next home. Now don't go getting any ideas while I go to her, Mia. Remember, I still have the gun, and your cop friend won't be able to run."

Disgust roils in my guts, but I keep it from my face as Father Donovan moves to the wooden door of the cell in the shadows of the basement, switching on an additional light to give him a better look. The door has no lock on it, only a simple deadbolt that he slides out of place to open the door.

The light shining into the cell gives me enough of an idea of the state of the girl inside the cell that the anger flaring in my chest has me almost choking.

Her wrists are still bound, and her mouth is taped; her left leg is shackled to a steel ring embedded in the floor. The dress she is wearing is filthy and somewhat torn and leaves little to the imagination. The dress was pretty, once upon a time, and must have looked incredibly lovely on her. There isn't much to the rest of the cell as it is incredibly small. The fear in her eyes tells me enough of what exactly Ethan and I had interrupted. I just hope we interrupted the bastard soon enough.

"Now, now, gorgeous. I cannot have you kicking the door and damaging my property," he says to the girl, all smiles and the rage roils in my gut as I realize that the *property* he is referring to is not the cell door. It's the girl herself.

I move my eyes from Father Donovan back to the girl, and the fear on her face has me wanting to reach out to her, bundle her in my arms, and run far away from here. But besides the fact that it won't work, I cannot leave Ethan here in this barn basement to bleed out.

I avert my eyes from the girl, the guilt of not being able to help her immediately like a physical pain in my heart, as I realize that Father Donovan has been watching my reaction to all of this. To the sight of her.

"Come on, Mia. You can show me how you feel. Aren't we friends? If you have something to say about my other guest here, just say it."

I look down, not sure that I can keep the disgust and anger from my face well enough to keep the ruse of submission going. Hopefully, Father Donovan thinks my inability to look him in the eyes is due to the fact that I am scared.

I need to dig deep and act like I have never acted in my life before. Not only my life but Ethan's life and the life of this young girl depend on it.

"I... I don't have anything to say. I just... I just want to know what you are doing here with all of this. And why here? I don't know of any connections you have to Cedarwood or any of the neighboring towns. Or am I wrong?"

Father Donovan snorts, turning his back to the girl in the cell, leaning against the cell door.

"Well, I guess I can tell you about my little operation here as you won't be leaving here voluntarily. You know, I can make quite a pretty penny selling you, Mia. Your face is mostly symmetrical, and that pretty mouth of yours is sexy. Your ass is nice and tight, perfect to slap, and your tits are a good handful," he remarks with a grin that verges on a sneer as he looks me up and down like a hunter assessing their prey. "There are men who would pay handsomely to have their way with you for a few hours. It's just a pity that beauty never lasts. The special medications needed to keep you women compliant take a toll after a while. And then, of course, some of our clients get a bit overexcited, damaging the goods in their pursuit of ecstasy. But ah, well. We must all make sacrifices for the greater good."

A thrill of fear goes through me at his words and the possibilities of what could await me if I am unable to stop him. I need to get closer to him. I need to keep him talking. Luckily, he seems to love his own voice. Somehow, I need him to be more comfortable in the situation. He needs to feel as though he is in total control and I won't be doing anything to stop him.

My mind races as I try to make sense of all the ways I can keep him feeling in control while still trying to get close to him. I look up at him, and his expression tells me he saw the thrill run through me. He knows exactly what his words did to me, what it made me think of, and he loves the control he has.

"I am sure you can appreciate that, as a businessman, I am always on the lookout for new live products to add to my catalog, and you would be a perfect addition. But, getting back to my little operation here, I decided on this quaint little town as it is on such an easy route from New York Harbor, and I can get my live products to any city in the south of the US fairly easily. From there, getting to any country in South America is child's play. And to be honest, I don't really care what happens after that. As long as I have my money, the live products can go wherever the buyer wishes to take them."

Kicking the girl's foot lightly with that feral wolfish grin on his face, he continues, "My live products, such as this one, come from China. So silly. A young girl going on vacation on her own in a foreign country. Visiting nightclubs, drinking, partying it up. All it takes is one small dose of the right drug in her drink, and I have my newest live product."

It is taking everything in me to keep the anger and disgust from showing on my face, but I have to do it as I look him in the eyes. I have to make sure I keep Father Donovan feeling in complete control. He needs to keep believing I am his compliant puppet.

"And... And your other... Products? I assume they do not come from China... rather, South America."

"Ah, the FBI Agent in you is on the case, I see. I have products coming from all over the world, to be honest. Drugs and weapons from South America. Uncut diamonds from a few African countries. It pays to have diversified interests. And if one route is shut down by the FBI, CIA, DEA, or some other organization determined to be a pain in my ass, my business won't suffer."

Father Donovan pushes away from the cell door, aiming for me.

"I grow tired of speaking, and I need to go untie the idiots upstairs at some point. I am going to tie you up now and put you in our other cell for live products, but don't try any funny business. I don't mind putting a few more holes in the pig over there." He motions to Ethan, and I have to fight the urge to look at Ethan over my shoulder. His breathing is labored and uneven, and I know another bullet would be the end of him.

"You, though, I want to keep in one piece as far as possible. Looking at you close up; you are much prettier than that pain in the ass sister of yours. She was so holier than thou it made me sick. Came running to me after she had sex for the first time to confess her sin. And interrupted me in the middle of an important business deal that I had to make at the motel. No one else was supposed to be there; Adam had arranged it so well. Until she showed up. That little *bitch*."

He stops right in front of me, so close that I can feel his breath on my face as he spits the last word out. The anger in that one word is enough to tell me that it had been a pleasure for him to kill Lily. But I need to play dumb. I need to get him to confess to me. I need the full story.

"Is that why you had Lily killed? Because she interrupted your meeting? Why not sell her to the highest bidder?"

"Come now, Mia, you know why. If I had put Lily on my inventory list and she escaped at some point, my operation would have been blown. She could identify me. And using someone from Cedarwood or the surrounding towns would be too easy to track if they got free somehow."

His one hand reaches up, and he caresses my cheek in a manner that tells me he wants me to know he has full control. He can touch me however and wherever he wants to.

"No, no, much better to keep the live products unrelated to my base of operations. And after she almost cost me the deal it was my pleasure, an absolute pleasure, to show my new associates how I handle issues. Luckily, your sister was so trusting that inviting her in to meet everyone so that I could explain how I was helping to save their souls helped me so much."

Father Donovan leans in closer, moving my hair behind my ear as he whispers to me.

"She didn't even try to scream for help when I closed my hands around her skinny little neck and squeezed. Watching the life drain out of her eyes..."

He pulls back to look me square in the eyes, his hand brushing down my chest, cupping my breast, traveling down my stomach before coming to rest on my waist.

"Ah, Mia, there is no feeling quite like it. Seeing your own strength. It is like having sex with a gorgeous woman and seeing her reach ecstasy at the same moment you do. Hmm... I am sure you don't need to be taught anything about that kind of pleasure, but perhaps one day you will enjoy the pleasure of taking a life because you can... because you want to."

# Chapter 21:

I am unable to keep the disgust from my face this time, and his victorious smile at this is enough to make the roaring in my ears return, threatening to drown out everything else. But before I can do or say anything, he removes his hand from my waist and motions to my belt.

"I see you have some zip ties on your belt. Take a pair out so that we can bind your hands. I want to get on with my day, even though I have had so much fun with you."

This is my chance, I realize as I remove the zip tie from my belt, pretending to be clumsy as I drop the zip tie.

"Sorry. I'm... I'm sorry. I didn't mean... mean to drop it," I stammer out in pretend fear as I bend down to pick up the zip tie I dropped strategically on my left.

Bending down, I make a show of fumbling for the zip tie with my left hand as my right-hand slides into my pant leg and I grab the hilt of the knife I have in my shoe.

"Sorry, I got it," I say as I stand up with the zip tie in my left hand. I keep the knife flat against the inside of my right arm, my hand in a fist around the hilt, hoping he is so convinced of his dominance that he won't notice my clenched right hand. "I just... I just can't put these on by myself. I need someone to pull the zip ties closed."

I hold the zip ties out to him while keeping my eyes down, the picture of defeat as Father Donovan sighs dramatically.

"First butterfingers, and now you cannot even do a simple task on your own. Tsk, Mia. What would the FBI think if they saw their little agent now?" he gloats as he puts his gun in his belt, exactly as I had hoped.

As he reaches for the zip tie, I angle my body slightly to draw my right arm back without him noticing immediately.

Zip tie in hand, he takes my left hand in his to slip the zip tie over and sees my angled body too late. He is too late to stop me.

Screaming, I flick my right arm up and slam the blade home in Father Donovan's neck, right up to the hilt, while I grab his gun from his belt with my left hand. Taking a few quick steps back, the gun now in my hands, I leave the blade buried in his neck. Blood starts leaking from the wound immediately, trickling down his neck as he falls to his knees in pain in front of me.

His face is a mask of surprise, shock, and pain as he reaches up to grab the knife, and I take a step back.

"I wouldn't do that if I were you, *Father*. If you remove the knife, you will bleed to death within a matter of minutes. But if you leave it in, you have a chance of surviving. If you can get medical assistance quickly enough."

The venom, hate, and fear in his eyes as he glares up at me is like a physical touch, and I relish it. Every second of it. Still glaring at me, he lets his hand drop from the knife hilt.

This piece of shit has killed countless people and ruined many more lives, and he deserves to die. But we need answers. And there are families out there who deserve to know what happened to their loved ones.

I also know other girls out there need to be found and brought back home.

No matter my feelings, Father Donovan needs to live in order for them to survive and be found.

"You bitch. I am going to make you pay for this."

He coughs, and a bit of blood trickles out of his mouth.

"Shut up, asshole. You're done. And the more you talk, the more your neck muscles move, and the knife will keep slicing you up from the inside. Try to use your one remaining brain cell to keep yourself alive."

I step closer to Father Donovan again and roughly help him up, dragging him to the stairs. Using the zip ties, I tie his hands and feet and secure him to the stairs. A quick pat down assures me that he has no other weapons on him, and his sheer arrogance hits me once again as I stare him down.

The knife hilt sticking out of his neck looks grotesque in a satisfactory way, and blood is leaking from it in a steady stream now, staining his shirt.

I realize that I still have a myriad of questions I want to ask Father Donovan, but a groan from Ethan is enough to break my attention away from the murderer in front of me.

I need to get Ethan out of here; then I can deal with this asshole. I turn back to Ethan. The color of his skin has me walking over to him with haste. He is pale, too pale. Can someone even survive this much blood loss?

Lifting his shirt, I assess the wound. The bullet wound is a through-and-through, and the exit wound at the front looks to be clean. But the bullet must have nicked an organ for the bleeding to be this bad. I need to bind it and stop the bleeding somehow.

Ethan is too heavy to move in his mostly unconscious state, and I feel a slight panic go through me. I need an extra set of hands to bind his wounds and to get him out of here; I need help.

Of course! The girl.

I whirl around so fast that I startle her, and it takes me a moment to remember that I need to be kind, gentle, and careful, no matter how urgently Ethan needs attention. She has been through way too much already, and putting any pressure on her now will not help the situation. Without her assistance, Ethan might not have made it out of this basement alive.

Taking a calming breath, I walk over to her, hands up, showing my open palms: a gesture of peace.

She might not understand English, which would make communication difficult, I realize belatedly. I will need to keep my wording as basic as possible until I can confirm whether she understands me or not.

"Hi, it's okay. It's okay. My name is Mia, and I am an FBI agent. I want to help you, but I need your help as well. To save my friend. He was shot," I say as I point to Ethan behind me. "I'm going to untie you now. Do you understand me?"

Her eyes are wide, fearful, but she nods in understanding.

I crouch down next to her in the filthy cell, reaching out to remove the duct tape from her mouth.

"This is going to hurt, sorry."

A bit of determination shines through in her eyes as she nods at me again, and I pull the duct tape off her mouth.

The flash of pain across her face is replaced by relief as she draws a big breath in through her mouth and licks her lips.

"Thank you so much. I was so scared no one would find me. And yes, I can help."

Her voice is sweet but slightly rough, most probably from screaming or from thirst. Perhaps a combination of both.

"I'm just glad we found you," I reply as I tear the duct tape on her wrists and take a look at the lock on the cuff around her ankle. The key. I need the key.

"He has the key," she says as she points to Father Donovan. "He took the duct tape off my feet, and then he…"

Her eyes flashing away from me to the corner tells me exactly what he planned to do next, and I nod my head in understanding so that she knows she does not need to continue talking if she can't.

I stand up to get the keys, and as I do, I ask her, "What's your name? I hear you have a French accent, so I am assuming you are from France?"

As I pat Father Donovan down for the keys, she clears her throat to answer.

"Oui, I am French, from Toulouse, and my name is Camille. I went to China on holiday like he said, and someone… They just took me. I don't know how long it's been since I was taken. I... I don't even know what day it is."

I leave her to talk as I unlock the cuff and remove it from her foot, hoping that she won't go deeper into shock before we get out of there.

"Don't worry, Camille. I have you now, and you are going to be okay. I just need you to help me with my friend, with Ethan, then we can get out of here. Can you stand?"

Standing up myself, I reach a hand towards her to help her up, and she gratefully takes it, pulling herself onto her feet. She seemed to be stable enough to stand and I beckoned her over to Ethan.

"I'm just grabbing what I can find for now to close Ethan's wound."

She nods at me, and I turn back to the basement area, scanning for anything that can be of help.

The roll of duct tape catches my eye, and I grab it. will work perfectly to hold pieces of Ethan's shirt in place over the wound.

I feel down Ethan's legs for a blade and find a knife strapped to his calf. It's exactly what I need to cut his shirt into pieces to use as a wound dressing.

Camille comes up to help me, and we make quick work of dressing the entry wound in Ethan's back before we turn him back over to deal with the exit wound that is now bleeding worse after the movement.

Her gasp at the sight of his wound bleeding so profusely tightens my heart.

"Will he be... okay? That is a lot of blood, Mia."

Focus, Mia.

Stay calm.

Focus.

"Yes, he will be fine. I just need to put pressure on the wound to relieve the bleeding. I just wish I had a tampon to put in the wound. It would help so much."

Where is that one emergency tampon at the bottom of my bag when I need it?

The useless thought has me suppressing a giggle.

My mind is clearly all over the place, but I need to focus.

"Camille, can you roll up a piece of the dressing we cut as tightly as possible and keep it ready for me? I need to put my finger inside the wound and see if I can find the source of the bleeding."

She nods grimly as I put my finger in the wound, the squelching sound loud enough to know I will be having nightmares about it.

I feel around but am unable to find anything that feels as though it might be the source of the bleeding. I cannot waste more time to get Ethan help, I will need to have blind faith that the plug will work.

I hold my hand out for the tightly rolled piece of dressing and Camille places it in my hand, ensuring that I have a good grip on it before she lets go.

"Okay, I'm going to remove my finger and quickly replace it with the dressing, and then I need you to put a piece of duct tape over the wound. Tightly, so that it mimics the pressure of my finger in the wound. Got it? Good. Then here we go."

I carefully extricate my finger from the wound and stuff the roll of dressing into the wound, and Camille immediately puts a piece of duct tape tightly over the wound and dressing.

The fact that Ethan has not woken up during any of this has me worried. He has lost too much blood, and we need help. Now.

The creaking of floorboards above us startles both me and Camille. Was I truly concentrating so hard that I did not even hear someone approaching?

I hastily remove the gun from my belt and shove Camille behind me, readying myself for whoever might be coming down the stairs at any moment.

"What the…? Mia? Ethan?"

The relief washing through me is enough to make my knees almost buckle as Kyle's voice reaches me.

"Kyle! We're down here! I need help, Ethan is injured," I shout up the stairs at Kyle, and I hope he will remember the basement.

His quick footstep approaching tells me he does remember, and I put the gun away, looking at Father Donovan and his paling face.

"Before anyone else arrives, before anything else happens, I want you to look at me and listen. Listen carefully. I am going to put you away for the rest of your life. You will rot and die in prison and never again be able to hurt anyone. Do you understand me? I will personally see to it and use every resource at my disposal to keep you locked up. You are a sick fucker who does not deserve to see the sun ever again."

As Kyle reaches the bottom of the stairs, his eyes go to Father Donovan first, taking in the blade in his neck and the zip ties keeping him in place. Kyle's eyes go wide as he takes in the rest: Camille in her filthy scraps, my hands full of blood, and Ethan lying on the steel crate.

Rushing for Ethan, Kyle says, "Shit, what happened here? Is she okay? And Ethan... Never mind. Here, Mia, use my phone and call an ambulance, and then get some more officers out here."

# Chapter 22:

The last 24 hours have been a blur in my mind.

I stifle a groan as I sit down on the couch in Ethan's house, a cup of decaf coffee in hand. Caffeine will just keep me awake unnecessarily tonight, and I do not need anything else disturbing my sleep. Enough terrors are running through my mind and "what ifs" plaguing my conscience.

The FBI agent across from me clears his throat to remind me of his presence, and I nod at him. For a moment, I completely forgot about him.

"Agent Conrad, as I was saying before, we were able to find evidence tying the man masquerading as Father Donovan to all the accidents you and Detective Hayes identified as murders, and we found bodies buried on the farm with DNA evidence tying them to the suspects as well. We were able to identify a few other players in the organization thus far, but we are still interviewing the suspects and combing through the photos you took at New York Harbor. We also found a recording device on Detective Hayes that contains the confession given to you by Jono Lowes regarding your sister's murder. It corroborates your statement of Lowes' confession in full, and it won't be only your word against his. He'll be in prison for the rest of his life, along with his accomplices."

The relief running through me at the confirmation of the evidence found has me almost breaking down into a puddle of tears.

But I hate crying. And this news is the type of news I celebrate, not shed tears over.

"Adam was arrested last night and has agreed to testify against Lowes in exchange for a deal, which will also help our case. He alleges that he can identify additional victims and can help find some of the women who have been trafficked. We are thus hopeful that at least a few more women can be found and returned to their homes."

He pauses, giving me a moment to interject if I want to, but I am too tired to add anything.

"If there is nothing further you have to add to your statement at present, I will be heading back to New York and leaving two agents here to liaise with the local authorities on the details of the case and to disband the illegal operation here in full. We have given a statement to the town's press about the details of the events, but, unfortunately, someone from the police department has leaked details regarding the blackmail files that were used on the victims, and emotions are running high in town. I would recommend you not leave the house for the rest of the day and possibly tomorrow as well. I am sure you can use the rest in any way."

Getting up, I nod absentmindedly.

As I walk Agent Fallon to the front door, he remarks, "Agent Conrad, good work on this case. I look forward to getting to know you better at the New York field office. I think your talents are wasted in Cyber Crime. Come see me if you ever want to get out from behind your desk."

Without waiting for an answer, Agent Fallon walks out of the front door and to his car, leaving me with more to think about.

Agent Fallon's words are still ringing in my mind as I slip into the hot bath, a glass of wine standing on the edge of the tub.

The visit to Ethan in the hospital felt much too short, but as he is still weak, I do not want to tax him too much. Kyle, at least, seemed like himself while visiting Ethan as well. He was reading through Ethan's medical charts when I came in and immediately updated me on Ethan, Camille, and Jono Lowes. Not that I cared too much about Lowes.

Ethan had suffered significant blood loss due to the period the wound had gone untreated, but the physical bleeding was not as terrible as it had looked to me (or so the medical professionals say; I still beg to differ), and they were able to patch up him fairly easily.

Camille is still in shock and will be kept in the hospital for another day or two, where she can start getting help to deal with what had been done to her. Luckily, her parents were located and were on their way to Cedarwood already. She gave me a big hug when I looked in on her, but I am not sure I deserved any of the thanks. She has been through so much, and Ethan and I did not interrupt quickly enough...

I shake my head, trying to rid myself of the thoughts threatening to overwhelm me. Logically, I know that I am not responsible for what happened to Camille in that basement, but the feelings in my heart don't always want to agree with my logical mind.

Kyle's update about Lowes was brief, as though he could also not stand speaking about the bastard for too long. No permanent damage from the knife in his neck, although Lowes will have a lovely scar to remember me by. In my weaker moments, I curse myself for not pulling out the knife and letting him bleed to death, but I know that is my anger speaking and that it would not have been true justice. Not the justice that all his victims deserve.

I swirl the bubbles in the bath with my hand, watching the patterns they make as the thoughts continue to run through my mind. It feels like just yesterday that I arrived in town but also, somehow, weeks ago, and I am sure I have aged at least ten years in the few days here.

I idly and without thinking reach up to touch my hair, wondering if there might be any gray hairs hiding somewhere. I sure earned a few. Perhaps I need a vacation, or to just work in my office only.

And yet...

I enjoyed the investigating, the physical work, the chase both behind and without a computer. It was definitely much more enjoyable and satisfying than simply handing the information over to a team and then sitting back. This time, I didn't have to wait for the guilty parties to be stopped, brought in, and held accountable for their actions; I stopped them and made sure they would be held accountable for their crimes.

Including killing Lily.

I have been careful not to think about her too much since we got out of that barn basement. Careful not to dig too deep into my feelings towards Father Donovan, Lowes, whatever his name is, for what he did to my sister.

Even more careful not to think about my parents.

But the thoughts are now crossing my mind, unwanted, as I take a sip of my wine. Wondering... Wondering if my parents will finally be proud of me. If Lily would finally be happy to have me as a sister because I brought her murderer to justice.

And I know, know in my heart, that the answer is "no," and I am okay with it.

The peace I found after leaving my parents in the coffee shop a few days ago (was that only a few days ago? Gods) is what I need to hold onto. I will never be Lily, never be the perfect daughter they had and lost, but I accept that and myself for who I am: a flawed human doing her best.

I smile to myself as the realization washes through me again. It might have taken me a few years, but I can finally accept myself, my past, and my present for what they are and work on a better future for myself.

And perhaps that future will include field work and physical investigations outside of my computer screen. And maybe... Maybe it will include some romance.

Ethan's face flashes through my mind, and I sigh into my wine glass.

As handsome as the detective is, perhaps he will be the one that I always wonder about. The one that got away.

I snort at the thoughts of romance and drain the last of my wine in a single swallow.

The bath water is getting cold, and my thoughts are running amok.

Time for one of those tablets Kyle gave me and some proper sleep.

# **Chapter 23:**

Ethan is so bloody pig-headed that I am just thankful he agreed to the wheelchair as we stop a few feet from Lily's grave, Kyle walking behind us.

We had decided to meet at Lily's grave today to bid her a final farewell and then go for coffee and brunch.

Unfortunately, my parents also decided to visit Lily's grave today, and their eyes turned to the three of us, standing a few feet away.

My father simply curtly nods at me, turning away with his hands in his pockets, but my mother walks closer, tears streaking her face.

"Mia. I…"

She swallows, carefully dabbing at her face with a tissue to not ruin her makeup while wholly ignoring Ethan and Kyle.

"Mia, your father and I just came to say goodbye to Lily before we left. We weren't sure we'd see you again, but… But I want to thank you for finding the people responsible for taking Lily from us. It… It helps to know they will no longer be walking around freely."

I try my best to keep my face neutral as surprise runs through me. Never, in a million years, would I have guessed that my mother, the woman who discarded me because I am an embarrassment to her, would thank me for finding Lily's killer.

I nod back at her, and, keeping my voice neutral, I reply, "I cannot say that it is a pleasure, but I'm glad that Ethan, Kyle, and I were able to find justice for Lily and the other victims."

My mother, looking at me like she is seeing me for the first time ever and blinking in surprise, simply nods. Without another word, she turns back to my father, and they walk off.

Kyle releases a breath behind me like he has been holding it in, startling me slightly.

"Well, I guess you never thought that would happen, hey, Mia? I only see it now, but your parents are, uhm, strange people. Especially your dad. Man."

The complete surprise in Kyle's voice has Ethan laughing, and I can't stop my own laughter from escaping.

"Kyle, please never change," I say to him through my laughing fit. "I need people like you in my life to remind me not to be so serious."

We left flowers at Lily's grave, and some piece of my heart is feeling much lighter than it has in years.

I smile with an ease I've never felt while in Cedarwood, and Ethan lifts an eyebrow at me over his cup of coffee, smiling back at me as though he knows exactly what I am feeling.

His skin is still much too pale for my liking, but no number of threats or pleading from Kyle, me, the other doctors, and nurses could keep Ethan in the hospital longer. Apparently, Mr. Otis cannot live on his own for too long… or that is the excuse he used to discharge himself from the hospital. No mention of me looking after Otis in the meantime and that Otis has not been alone the last few days.

"So, Mia, what's next for you? Back to New York?" Kyle inquires as he watches the exchange of looks between Ethan and me.

"Yes, I am actually leaving today, in a bit. My car is packed, Otis already got his goodbye hug and treats, and I just need to have a last Raven Diner coffee and brunch with two weird men who won't let me just slip away unseen, and then I'll be off."

Ethan and Kyle both laugh at my attempt at a joke, but the laugh does not fully reach Ethan's eyes. I wonder what that is about.

"Well, you are more than welcome to come and visit any time, Mia. There will always be a place for you to stay here in town if you want."

Kyle's offer is genuine, but I know I won't ever be making use of it. Still, I smile and nod at him as we are interrupted by the server bringing our food to the table.

"And hey, you need to keep in touch with Ethan and me. We didn't just go through all of this so that you can ghost us. Now, where's the ketchup?"

# Chapter 24:

The ride back home to New York had been filled with music and random thoughts running through my mind.

I had said goodbye to Kyle outside of the Raven Diner, and the hug he gave me surely bruised a rib or two.

Ethan had insisted that he could get home on his own, but I had rolled my eyes at him, bullied him into my car, and dropped him at home.

He had been... Different, softer, when I said goodbye. He had simply stood up out of the wheelchair right in front of me, against me, looked me in the eyes, and brushed a stray strand of hair out of my face. I wasn't sure if I should say something... if I even *could* say anything. My hesitation must have shown on my face, as his only reaction was to bend down and kiss me on the cheek. Gently, like he was afraid I would break.

"Mia," was all he said, before he turned around and pushed the wheelchair up the path to his front door, not even giving me the chance to say goodbye.

So typical, was all I could think as I shook my head and turned back to my car.

And now, here I am, driving back into New York City. I am almost home. Only another hour, and I will be able to sink into my own bed to sleep and find oblivion for a few hours.

I hope Angie remembered to water my plants, but I guess I will know that soon enough.

I am amazed to find that my office looks exactly the same as I had left it, and I shake my head at myself for the thought. Why would anything be different?

I unpack my laptop and rewire everything on my desk to be connected. External screens, speakers, charger, wireless keyboard, and mouse: all back in their places, all where I need them.

"Mia, welcome back!" Angie exclaims as she walks into my office. Her role as superior is forgotten for the moment, it seems. "Sorry I didn't call you last night, but I thought you could use the sleep. Agent Fallon told me about everything that had happened in Cedarwood and the good work you did. I am thoroughly impressed and a little pissed that you did not call me when things had somewhat settled after you arrested that fake preacher."

I smile at Angie and her compliment and admonishment that she has rolled all into one.

"I missed you, too, Angie. Thank you, I'm just glad I could find the responsible parties. And I am sorry for not phoning you. Everything was a bit of a blur, and I knew I would be seeing you soon. It is much more fun to inform you of everything over a good bowl of pasta and a good Cab Sav."

Angie's eyes soften as she nods at my words, a smile on her face.

"Very well, I accept your apology. "Now, tell me," she says as she closes my office door behind her. "How are you feeling? And what happened with your parents? I understand from Agent Fallon that they were in town while you were there. He spoke to them about Lily and informed them of Lowes' arrest, but he says they seemed to not even react to you being the one that found the bastard. I guess some people never change, do they?"

The dryness in Angie's voice at the last part has me stifling a smile, and I launch into an account of the events in Cedarwood and how I have been coping. I tell Angie about meeting my parents in the Raven Diner, speaking to them for the first time in years, and the realization I came to after the meeting. I tell her everything, including about Ethan and Kyle, and I can see the questions burning in her, but she keeps quiet until the end.

"I know I won't ever go back to Cedarwood, but it was kind of Kyle to invite me to visit. I would honestly rather he visits here."

Angie seems to have swallowed all her questions as her face turns pensive.

"You know, Mia, with all the information gathered, a massive smuggling ring has been disbanded, and we have been able to follow the trail and apprehend so many other criminals. You should be proud of the work you did."

"Hm, yes, I am. It is just... It still bothers me. The MicroSD card I received... You couldn't trace who gave it to the delivery person, and I found no other information on the card itself to tell me where it might have come from. Who sent it to me, and why? The only reason I can think of is that a rival gang wanted me, us, to take down this operation so that they could move in on the territory. I don't know..."

A knock on the door interrupts me, and O'Donnell steps into my office without invitation.

"Hey, boss," he says to Angie, "sorry to interrupt, but a package just arrived for our hero over here."

He indicates to me with his head, the only acknowledgment of my presence.

"Thanks, O'Donnell. You can leave it on my desk."

I cut him off before he can say anything else, and I hope he will remove himself from my office without further fuss.

"Sure, Conrad, here you go."

He tosses the package onto my desk in front of me, flashing a grin at Angie before exiting.

But I don't even register this as I pick up the envelope in front of me.

It is the same type of envelope that was sent to me with the MicroSD card that helped me solve Lily's murder. This time, though, there is writing on the envelope. It's written in the same script I found on the scanned page on the MicroSD card.

*Ready to test your luck again, Mia?*
*I know you missed me.*

# Shrouded Deception

## Hacking Dark Secrets in Riverview

Thank you for reading Shattered Echoes and I hope you enjoyed the story of FBI Agent Mia Conrad. Feel free to leave a review if you like, it would be greatly appreciated!

## Shrouded Deception:

**On the watch list of the FBI, a skilled hacker in her late twenties, Alex Harper, is unexpectedly drawn into her past.**Her childhood friend, Olivia Sinclair, vanishes under mysterious circumstances. Alex is thrust into a realm of deception, danger, and unforeseen alliances. Only to uncover a network of high-profile individuals with dark secrets. As well as some of her own... She must team up with the local Detective Adrian and the bad boy Max from her past. Together, this trio must navigate Riverview's dark underbelly. Exposing a web of deceit, coverups, and long-buried grudges along the way. As the body count rises, the trio faces threats from the unexpected. They are forced to question the loyalty of those closest to them. Alex's journey takes a personal turn when she receives a series of encrypted messages. What is the link between Olivia's disappearance and a traumatic event from her past?

## Shrouded Deception:

Chapter 1

*Present day...*

The sound of dirt hitting the wooden lid rouses me. My brain and body compete to figure out where I am, but there's only darkness. The voices gradually drift in as mounds of dirt hit the wood like a hailstorm.

I start to panic, and I know from experience that panicking won't help. I slowly try to work out the dimensions of the box in my head.

A searing pain tears through my right side as I lift my hands to push against the top. I wince uncontrollably and touch my head with my left hand. I can feel the lukewarm, sticky liquid beginning to clot on the side of my head. I try to remember what happened and where I am, but nothing comes to me. The only thing I know is that I have to get out of here.

I hear the voices fade. The lid gives way a little. It's not a coffin but feels more like a box. I consider kicking against it but realize that the noise will attract too much attention. Whoever is doing this has no fear of time or being caught. Leaving in the middle of burying someone alive isn't smart, but they must think that I'm dead.

Dirt falls into the box as I push against it, and I need to control myself again as I taste blood. The dirt in my mouth causes panic to rise from the pit of my stomach. After a few shoves, I figure out that something is keeping the lid in place. A lock? I try to stay calm as I contemplate my next move.

Should I scream? Maybe there's some humanity left in whoever's doing this, and hearing that I'm still alive will make them rethink their plan. Unlikely. Anyone who can come this far is likely to want to cover their tracks, and if that means hastily shoveling the remaining sand on me, so be it. Think, Alex! Think! I trace my way down the opening to find the chain or bolt that's keeping me trapped in here. I find it and try to make out what it is through touch in the pitch dark.

Download Shrouded Deception now to keep reading...

# Don't miss out!

Visit the website below and you can sign up to receive emails whenever Stella Mace publishes a new book. There's no charge and no obligation.

https://books2read.com/r/B-A-KHASB-DXNPD

**BOOKS 2 READ**

Connecting independent readers to independent writers.

www.ingramcontent.com/pod-product-compliance
Lightning Source LLC
Chambersburg PA
CBHW050522160726
48003CB00001B/422